A De___

"If you capture Schneck ___
of five ___
to Mr. ___

"I h___
Gara___

"Dic___

"No___

"The___

"Ha___
to me," ___

"Tel___

"Snake Eyes," Garaboxosa said. "Look at the barrels.

He set the shotgun on the floor butt-first, and Brad stared
at the twin muzzles. They were dark and ominous, like eyes
that could kill.

SNAKE EYES

A SIDEWINDER NOVEL

JORY SHERMAN

BERKLEY BOOKS, NEW YORK

THE BERKLEY PUBLISHING GROUP
Published by the Penguin Group
Penguin Group (USA) Inc.
375 Hudson Street, New York, New York 10014, USA
Penguin Group (Canada), 90 Eglinton Avenue East, Suite 700, Toronto, Ontario M4P 2Y3, Canada
(a division of Pearson Penguin Canada Inc.)
Penguin Books Ltd., 80 Strand, London WC2R 0RL, England
Penguin Group Ireland, 25 St. Stephen's Green, Dublin 2, Ireland (a division of Penguin Books Ltd.)
Penguin Group (Australia), 250 Camberwell Road, Camberwell, Victoria 3124, Australia
(a division of Pearson Australia Group Pty. Ltd.)
Penguin Books India Pvt. Ltd., 11 Community Centre, Panchsheel Park, New Delhi—110 017, India
Penguin Group (NZ), 67 Apollo Drive, Rosedale, Auckland 0632, New Zealand
(a division of Pearson New Zealand Ltd.)
Penguin Books (South Africa) (Pty.) Ltd., 24 Sturdee Avenue, Rosebank, Johannesburg 2196,
South Africa

Penguin Books Ltd., Registered Offices: 80 Strand, London WC2R 0RL, England

This is a work of fiction. Names, characters, places, and incidents either are the product of the author's imagination or are used fictitiously, and any resemblance to actual persons, living or dead, business establishments, events, or locales is entirely coincidental. The publisher does not have any control over and does not assume any responsibility for author or third-party websites or their content.

SNAKE EYES

A Berkley Book / published by arrangement with the author

PRINTING HISTORY
Berkley edition / December 2011

Copyright © 2011 by Jory Sherman.
Cover illustration by Bill Angresano.
Cover design by Lesley Worrell.
Interior text design by Laura K. Corless.

ISBN: 978-0-425-24487-6

BERKLEY®
Berkley Books are published by The Berkley Publishing Group,
a division of Penguin Group (USA) Inc.,
375 Hudson Street, New York, New York 10014.
BERKLEY® is a registered trademark of Penguin Group (USA) Inc.
The "B" design is a trademark of Penguin Group (USA) Inc.

PRINTED IN THE UNITED STATES OF AMERICA

10 9 8 7 6 5 4 3 2 1

For Michael Miller

ONE

~

Harry Pendergast, head of the Denver Detective Agency, located in a suite of the Brown Palace Hotel, looked up from the copy of the *Rocky Mountain News* when his secretary, Byron Lomax, entered his office without knocking. Byron was a small, thin man with skeletal features, and the skin on his face was stretched taut over a bony armature that gave him the gaunt look of a man who had missed too many meals.

Pendergast looked up from his paper, a shadow of annoyance on his face. His coffee cup sat in front of him, within easy reach, small streamers of steam edging over its rim.

"What is it, Lomax?" Pendergast said, his eyes floating above his tortoiseshell spectacles where they had slid to a point just behind the tip of his nose.

"Sir, there is a man waiting to see you. He says it is very urgent. He is quite insistent."

"Everything is urgent, Byron. What's his case?"

"I don't know, sir. He says he will only talk to you. The

way he put it was he would only speak to my chief. He has an accent. He might be a Mexican."

"Well, does he look as if he has money?"

"No, sir. He is wearing a suit, but it appears to be somewhat threadbare."

"Oh, all right, Byron, let him cool his heels for five minutes, then show him in. Did he tell you his name?"

"He did, sir, but . . ."

"Never mind. I'll find out about him pretty quick."

"Yes, sir, you are the detective, after all."

"Don't smart-mouth me, Lomax."

"Yes, sir," Lomax said, and he scurried from Pendergast's office like some furtive animal.

Pendergast lifted off his eyeglasses and set them atop the newspaper. He got out of his chair and stood up, walking to the round window behind his desk. He looked at the distant range of the Rocky Mountains, their peaks mantled in fresh snow, the foothills shining an emerald green in the sun. It was April and the mountain passes would still be blocked with snow, the spring runoff not yet swelling the South Platte, the Cache la Poudre, and the thousands of other streams that fed into the Arkansas and El Rio Grande del Norte.

He looked at Longs Peak. Its massive face was a brilliant white, clear to its base, glistening like some majestic edifice built by some ancient god. Denver basked in the glory of the Rockies, its streets and avenues muddy from rain and filled with morning traffic, buggies, wagons, horses, people dressed warmly against the gusts that bore the frosty chill of spring zephyrs.

Pendergast pulled on his watch fob, dipped it from his vest pocket. He cracked open the gold case and marked the time of day. He saw that four minutes had passed. He watched the second hand creep around the face and with five seconds left of the five minutes, he closed the lid and dropped the watch back into its pocket. He turned toward the door as it opened.

Byron Lomax ushered in the client and announced in a businesslike tone: "Mr. Pendergast, this is Mr. Garaboxosa to see you."

"Very well, Lomax," Pendergast said. "Please close the door."

Pendergast reached across his desk and held out his hand. Garaboxosa squeezed it so hard the blood vessels contracted and Pendergast winced. The swarthy man's hand was rough with calluses and scars.

"Have a chair, Mr. . . ."

"I am called Garaboxosa. Mikel Garaboxosa. You can call me Mike."

Pendergast sat down and Mike scooted a chair up to the opposite side of the desk, facing the detective, and plopped into it.

"What can I do for you, Mike?" Pendergast said, assuming an air of informality as he leaned back in his chair. He rubbed a hand over one cheek. His barber had scraped away his muttonchops the day before, and Pendergast was still unused to having a naked face.

"I want to hire you to find an assassin," Garaboxosa said. "There is a man who murdered my cousin, Eladio Zuniga."

"Isn't this a matter for the police, Mike?"

Garaboxosa shook his head, flaring his long dark locks that framed a moon face with a chin stippled with a two-day stubble of black-and-white beard. He wore a checkered woolen shirt under an unbuttoned sheepskin-lined leather jacket as well as a faded red cap with loose earflaps. His trousers were wrinkled and stained with dark unknown substances.

"I have been to the police. They will not help me."

"Why?"

"Ah, you ask the good question, Mr. Pendergast. When I tell them I am a rancher of sheep, they jump away from me as if I had leprosy."

"You're a sheep rancher, then?"

"Yes, from Wyoming. But we bring our flocks into the high country of Jefferson Territory where they can fatten on the good grass."

"So, who is the assassin of your cousin? Do you know who killed him? Do you have any proof?"

"I know without knowing, Mr. Pendergast."

"I'm afraid I don't understand, Mr. Garaboxosa."

"I did not see the one who murdered poor Eladio, but there was brutality after he was shot in the back."

"Brutality? On a corpse?" Pendergast picked up his eyeglasses, folded them up, and slipped them into the inside pocket of his coat. He drank more coffee as if to clear his mind.

"When we found Eladio, his head was gone, cut off at the neck. In its place was the head of a sheep. We found the sheep and my cousin's head was stuffed into its neck. It was plain to me who had assassinated my poor cousin."

"It was? I—I don't understand how you could come to any conclusion concerning the murderer at all."

"In the valley where we graze our sheep, there is competition from cattle. In another valley, a man grazes a large herd of cattle. Some of these cattle stray into our valley. This man told me last year not to drive my herd of sheep into this valley. He said that if I did, it would mean war."

"War?"

"That is the word that this man used, yes."

Garaboxosa touched a finger to a spot below his eye where a single tear had strayed. He wiped the moisture away and stiffened in his chair. His dark eyes narrowed and glowed like mirrored coals as the sunlight caught them in a snare of sprayed light.

"Jefferson Territory, this place they are calling Colorado," Pendergast said, "is cattle country. Sheep are a rarity, and I'm afraid there is deep hostility toward sheepmen among the cattle ranchers."

"That hostility has touched me and my fellows," Garaboxosa said. His eyes widened and turned black with suppressed rage. "I found the valley first, Mr. Pendergast. For two years now, we have been grazing our sheep in that same place. We have made camps and we have put up houses below the valley. We have brought our wives and children to the mountains and we have lived in peace."

"It seems to me that this is a private matter between you and the cattlemen. I don't see the need of a detective agency to solve your problem."

"This cattleman, the one who murdered Eladio, left a written note in my cousin's pocket. It said that we would all die unless we removed our sheep from the mountains."

"Do you have the note?" Pendergast asked.

Garaboxosa reached into his pocket and pulled out a scrap of wrinkled brown paper. He handed it across the desk to Pendergast.

The note was written in red ink, ink the color of blood. Pendergast read the words of warning.

"There is no signature," he said. "What is that at the bottom? A drawing of some sort. It looks like a snake. A rattlesnake, I presume. Very crude."

"It is a drawing of a snake with rattles," Garaboxosa said. "See the forked tongue, the swirls of the tail?"

"Yes, I see those things."

"The man who threatened me is a German. His name is Otto Schneck. His men call him 'Snake.'"

"Snake?"

"Yes, we have heard the cowboys call him by that name."

"What do you want my agency to do, Mr. Garaboxosa?"

The Basque sheepman steeled his jaw and leaned forward in his chair.

"I want you to follow this man and catch him, bring him to justice. I am prepared to pay with a generous sum of money. In advance."

Pendergast watched as Garaboxosa pulled an oblong wallet from his back pocket. The wallet was bulging with greenbacks.

"Here is two thousand dollars," Garaboxosa said and laid the stack of bills on Pendergast's desk.

Pendergast whistled when he saw the money. He picked it up and saw bills in two denominations: fifties and hundreds.

"That's a great deal of money, sir," Pendergast said.

"We are serious, Mr. Pendergast. We wish to hire you to remove this snake from our midst."

Pendergast leaned back in his chair. He fanned the bills and listened to the crisp rustle of money.

"I might have just the man to investigate your case, Mr. Garaboxosa."

"Yes?"

"Yes. His name is Brad Storm. He is a cattle rancher, but he is also a tough man who believes in justice. Funny thing is, they call him Sidewinder."

"What is this 'sidewinder' name?"

"A sidewinder is a snake, sir. A rattlesnake."

Garaboxosa let out a breath of air.

"Ah," he said. "It sounds like justice. You send a rattlesnake to kill a rattlesnake, no?"

Pendergast smiled and thumbed the money again. It made a sound like the whisper of a rattlesnake's tail.

"Exactly," he said.

TWO

❦

Brad Storm rode down to the foothills above Leadville in late afternoon. He wore buckskins over red flannel long johns to ward off the chill. The pale fire of the sun washed the bleak sky through thin scrims of high clouds. He headed for the wide, sheltered valley that had provided winter quarters for his cattle herd. He rode Ginger, a strawberry roan gelding with a white blaze flared on his forehead.

There were still streamers and clumps of snow in the wind-stunted scrub pines that stood on tiptoe among the crags of limestone that bordered the valley. Water ran into a natural catch basin where some of the cattle were drinking. They made burbling sounds with their rubbery lips as they blew and chaffed with their noses and muzzles. On one side of the valley, a creek flashed diamonds in the sun from every wave crest as it hurtled downward from twelve thousand feet where the snows were deep but had begun to melt in the day's sun.

In the far reaches of the valley, some cattle were lying down, resting in the shade of the limestone outcroppings.

Storm saw a man on horseback emerge from a shallow, brush-choked draw, driving a yearling calf ahead of him and his horse.

Brad lifted a hand and waved. He recognized the horseman as his foreman, Julio Aragon. He prodded Ginger's flanks with his blunt spurs and began closing the distance between them. Julio waved back and turned his horse.

The two men met near the upper part of the valley. Ginger whickered and Julio's horse, Chato, a pinto, nickered in reply.

"*Hola, Jefe*, how did you find the ranch? Is there snow on the ground?"

"You get right to the point, don't you, Julio?"

Julio grinned. He had the high cheekbones of the Indian race in his blood, the skin taut and faintly redolent of vermilion as if he bore the faint traces of war paint. His black eyes twinkled like sun-shot agates whenever he turned his head to catch the radiant streaks of the afternoon light. His hair was long and black, curly as ebony shavings from a carpenter's plane.

"The cattle, they look to the mountains every day. They wish to chew on long grass again."

Brad laughed.

"Homesick cattle? Maybe," he said. "Well, most of the snow has melted, and there is inch-high grass between the creeks. The creeks are running full and flowing onto the land on both sides. I think we can drive the herd back very soon. I saw elk heading for the high country, and you could count ribs under their hides."

"Then, we go as soon as we can get the men," Julio said. "I will tell those who wait in town."

"A day or two ought to do it. I just hope there won't be a late snow."

"It is not late for snow in the mountains, Brad."

"I know."

Julio stood up in the stirrups, looked over Brad's head, toward the road to Leadville. His eyes widened, and he waved.

Brad turned and saw a woman riding toward them.

"How does a woman know?" he asked. "They must be born with some kind of sixth sense."

"They can hear the talk in your mind," Julio said.

"Sometimes Felicity knows what I am thinking before I say anything, Julio."

Both men laughed.

"The horses, too, they read your thoughts, I think."

Brad waved to his wife, and she put her horse, Rose, a bottom-heavy bay mare, into a slow gallop.

Felicity was a slim, wiry woman with a patrician nose set in the center of sculptured facial features. She bore an expression of excitement on her face, and her hazel eyes sparkled with sunlight and an inner fire.

"You just get back, Brad?" she asked in an almost breathless voice.

"Minutes ago," he said.

She rode up close, leaned from her saddle, and gave him a peck on the cheek.

Then, she drew a folded piece of paper from her shirt pocket. She wore a mackinaw blouse, with a yellow scarf tied around her neck. Unlike many women of her day, she wore tight gabardine trousers cut to fit snugly to her hips and legs. Her feet were encased in kid boots that expressed their smallness and daintiness.

"Pendergast sent this note by messenger, so I hurried up here, hoping you'd be back from our ranch," she said.

She handed the note to Brad.

He read it quickly and his facial features hardened into an intense look of anger by the time he had read Pendergast's signature.

"He wants me to come to Denver right away," he said, a bitter edge to his voice.

"I know," she said. "He doesn't say why."

"He never does. 'Most urgent,' he says."

"I wonder what it is?" she said.

Julio looked at both of them but said nothing.

"I'm sorry I got roped into this detective business," he said.

"Do you have to go?" she said.

"I guess so. I gave my word that he could call on me when he needed to."

Felicity's face rumpled up as she fought back tears and tried to quell her disappointment.

"Hell," he said, "I've ridden all day, with Ginger picking his way through snowdrifts and muddy ground, so I guess I can ride to Denver. I can down a cup of strong coffee and chew on some grub while I ride."

"Surely you won't leave right now," she said, her eyes squinched to keep from weeping.

"Honey, 'right away' means right away. Harry even underlined those words."

"Oh, damn him," Felicity said, then clamped a hand over her mouth.

"He paid for these cattle, darlin'," Brad said. "I owe the man."

Felicity took in a deep breath and sat up straight, the anguish on her face a mere shadow as she composed herself.

"Brad Storm," she said, "one of these days you're going to have to decide whether you're a cattle rancher or a detective. You can't sell your soul to Harry Pendergast. The price is just too dear."

"We shook hands on it, Felicity."

"Oh, you men and your damned code of honor. Harry snaps his fingers and you come running."

"My obligation to him won't last forever, honey."

"It's lasted too long already," she snapped.

"When I see him, I'll tell Harry I won't do any more detective work," Brad said.

"Promise?"

"I promise," he said.

"I have your word on that, Brad?"

"Yes, honey. You have my solemn word."

She reached back and opened one of her saddlebags. She

pulled out a bulky package wrapped in butcher paper and tied with twine. She handed it over to her husband.

"I can't give you hot coffee," she said, "but there's more than enough food in there to get you to Denver."

Brad took the package in one hand, lifted it to his face. He smelled it.

"Roast beef sandwiches," she said.

"Better than the jerky and hardtack I've been chewing on for the past three days," he said. He slipped the food package into his saddlebag.

"You can stop in Leadville for coffee, maybe," she said.

"No, I'll ride the shortcut to Denver. Can't be any worse than what I've just been through."

He turned to Julio.

"So can you take the herd up in a day or two, Julio?"

"Yes. I will call the men back tonight and we can drive the cattle up maybe tomorrow or the next day."

"There's no hurry. Just so you're up there when I get back."

"When will that be?" Felicity asked.

"Three days at the most," he said.

"Are you going to quit when you see him or after you do the job he asks you to do?" Her words were blunt fists that he could not easily ward off.

"I can't promise to do it right off, darling. First, I'll hear what Harry has to say."

"What if . . . ?"

He waved her to silence.

"We won't be speculating on what I'll run into in Denver," he said. "I'll decide when I hear what Harry has to say."

"Write me what he says, Brad."

"You'll be at the hotel?" Pendergast had arranged for Storm to have permanent rooms at the hotel. It was where Felicity stayed when she had to spend a night or two away from the ranch.

"For a week or so. I'll expect you back sometime within the week, and we can ride up to the ranch together."

"I'll write you as soon as I know anything. And, if luck is with me, I'll beat the mail stage back to Leadville."

She reached over and grasped his arm. She squeezed it and looked into his blue eyes.

"Hurry back," she said.

He wanted to take her into his arms just then and hold her tight. A lump appeared in his throat and he couldn't speak for a moment or two. He patted her arm.

"I'll get back as quick as I can," he rasped, and she knew he was on the verge of tears, just as she was.

"Good-bye, Brad," she said and withdrew her hand from his arm. "Stay safe, no matter what."

"I will," he said.

"Vaya con Dios," Julio said.

"Adios, Julio," he said.

Brad rode out of the valley with Felicity, and they parted ways as she continued on into town. Brad did not look back, but he knew Julio would take one last check on the herd before riding into Leadville to round up hands for the drive up to the ranch.

The road to Denver was deserted and the western sky was ablaze with a golden sunset that shimmered beyond the snow-flocked peaks of the Rockies. The blue sky looked like the grand vault of a great cathedral as vaporous rays of light fanned out above the clouds and burned with that pale fire of heavenly origin.

He rode into darkness and descended into the glittering highway of stars and planets that formed the Milky Way.

He wondered, not what lay ahead on the road to Denver but what lay ahead in Pendergast's office and mind.

He did not dread the empty black road but the something that was "most urgent" awaiting him when he arrived in Denver.

Some triggered instinct deep inside him told him he would not be coming back in a few days as he had hoped. Harry had sent a messenger, a courier, instead of one of his agents.

That meant he was hiding something, and he didn't want Brad to know too much about the assignment until he was snared in Pendergast's web. Whatever Harry wanted, it was damned serious, and Brad felt like a condemned man riding toward a gallows tree, his hands tied behind his back.

And his eyes blindfolded.

THREE

❧

Brad's eyes burned in the gaudy glare of the lamps in Pendergast's office. The lids felt as if they were leaden. Every bone in his body ached and his buttocks were so tender he did not sit down when Harry offered him a chair. Denver was dark outside the office window, its streets a-flicker with a few gas-lit streetlamps. The mountains were a black shadow on the distant horizon, broken only by their dim blanched peaks, faint beacons in the moon and starlight that glittered under a blanket of billions of snow crystals.

Pendergast pulled open a drawer in his desk and took out a stack of bills. He laid them in the center of his empty desk.

Brad halted his pacing, rubbed his eyes for the dozenth time and stared at the money.

"There's one thousand dollars there," Pendergast said. "And our client, a sheepherder, will pay you a bonus when you have completed your assignment. He will be up here soon to confirm our agreement. I sent Lomax to fetch him."

"Harry, I rode four days without sleep to get here and you want me to work for a sheepherder. I'm a cattleman in case you didn't notice."

"I know, Brad, but this is a big case, and the man needs our help."

"You have other agents. I'm in the middle of moving my herd off of winter quarters and up to the ranch."

"A thousand dollars, Brad. In advance. I'll send it to Felicity by messenger, along with your letter to her, the one you wrote when you got here. My courier will beat the stage by at least a day."

"Do I get any help?"

"The client has men who will help you."

"Let me get this straight, Harry. You want this German cowpoke arrested for murder, right?"

"That would be ideal."

Brad flexed the fingers on both of his hands. They were stiff and wooden after the long ride.

"I'll hear what your client has to say and then I'll make my decision," Brad said.

"Fair enough. He should be here any minute now. He's staying here in the hotel."

"I may be asleep on my feet when he comes in."

"You won't want to sleep when you hear what this man has to say."

"He's a Basque, you say. From Wyoming."

"That's right."

"Why doesn't he take his flock back to Spain? A Wyoming sheepherder, for crying out loud."

Harry did not reply. The door opened and Mikel Garaboxosa entered the room, followed by Byron Lomax.

"Here they are," Harry said, his eyes bright and a big smile on his face.

Garaboxosa walked straight to where Brad stood and looked up at the man in buckskins. At six feet, Brad towered over him; he was even taller with his boots on. Brad looked down at the hatless man with tousled hair, coal black eyes, and swarthy features.

"So, you are the Sidewinder, eh? Lomax has bragged about you ever since he woke me up."

"I'm Brad Storm."

"I am Mike Garaboxosa. Do you know the Cache la Poudre country?"

"I know it," Brad said. He had fished it, waded across it on horseback, admired its power and energy when it tumbled and flowed over the large boulders strewn along its length.

"Good. We will ride there tomorrow. The main herds have not come down yet, but there are a few sheep we brought and little houses where we camp."

"I'm a cattleman, Mr. Garaboxosa," Brad said.

"Then you are perfect for the job."

"He doesn't know why you came here, Mike," Harry said. "This might be a good time to tell him what happened to your cousin. Brad, why don't you sit down and listen to what Mike has to say."

"If I sit down, I might fall asleep," Brad said.

"You won't sleep through this, Brad," Pendergast said. "Trust me."

"Yes, sit down, Mr. Sidewinder," Mike said. He gently guided Brad to the leather couch and pulled up a chair so that he sat close. Lomax drifted to a chair against a wall decorated with official documents and Pendergast's coat-of-arms plaque.

Garaboxosa leaned toward Brad and began to speak before Brad could protest.

His story was riveting to Brad, Harry, and Byron, all of whom listened in total silence to the gory account of the beheaded man who had a sheep's head placed where his head had been, atop his torso.

Brad cringed inwardly at the graphic description of the murdered man who had been transformed into some strange

kind of beast. He felt the passion of the Basque sheepman as
he told how the German, Otto Schneck, had threatened him.
His blood boiled at the injustice of the murder and the sorrow
it had caused Garaboxosa and the other sheepmen and their
wives and children.

Lomax wiped tears from his eyes.

Pendergast cleared the lump in his throat.

Brad no longer felt sleepy nor tired. He sat up straight and
shook his head. He took off his hat and wiped the sweat from
his forehead. His blue eyes blazed in the yellow spray of
lamplight.

"I am sorry for your loss, Mr. Garaboxosa," Brad said.

"You call me Mike, eh?"

"Mike," Brad said, a wry curl to his lips

"Then you will come with me to the mountains?"

"I will," Brad said. "Somebody's got to take this Schneck
down a notch or two."

Pendergast brightened as Garaboxosa offered his hand to
Brad and the two shook hands.

Then Harry walked to a large cabinet and opened it.

"I have a present for you, Brad. I bought it from my gunsmith this morning, at Mike's suggestion. I hope you like it."

Brad turned his head to see what Harry was taking out of
the tall cabinet.

Pendergast carried the object over to the couch and handed
it to Brad. It was a black leather sheath polished to a high
sheen, out of which jutted the polished curly maple stock of
a sawed-off shotgun. Brad pulled the double-barreled weapon
from its boot and stared with wide eyes at the cross-hatched
pair of hammers, the graceful trigger, and the bluing on the
barrel that shone with a lustrous glow as he turned it in the
lamplight. There was no front sight, nor a rear one. This was
a gun for killing man or beast at close range.

Harry reached down and picked up a box of shot shells.
He handed them to Brad.

"Double-ought buckshot," he said.

"It's a beautiful weapon, Harry," Brad said, still stunned at the gift. "But why? Why give me this gun?"

"It's a Greener, but my gunsmith filed down the sear. Those are hair triggers. Just a slight pull will set it off."

"In the mountains," Garaboxosa said, "we all carry these short shotguns because there are many trees and snakes, wolves that come after the sheep, and sometimes the bears and the mountain lions. We have the long rifles, too, but we use the shotguns when the danger is close or prowling among the pines and the junipers."

Brad set the gun and its case down and reached into his pocket. He pulled out a folded letter and held it out to Pendergast.

"Here's my letter to Felicity, Harry. Will you send a note that I won't be back home for a while? And, don't read what I said to her. It's private. Between man and wife."

"I won't look at it, Brad. And I'll write Felicity a nice note explaining that you are on a special case that might keep you here for several days."

Garaboxosa grinned.

Lomax sniffled as his tears dried up and stopped flowing.

"Do you need any ready cash before you go, Brad?" Pendergast asked as he strode to his desk.

Brad shook his head.

"I expect Mike will feed me and give me a place to lay out my bedroll, right, Mike?"

"You will not need money. But if you capture Schneck or kill him, I will pay you a bonus of five hundred dollars. Just to you, Brad. Not to Mr. Pendergast."

"I hope I don't have to kill him, Mike."

Garaboxosa reached over and picked up the shotgun.

"Did you tell him the name of the gun, Harry?" he asked.

"No, thought you might do that, Mike."

"The shotgun has a name?" Brad asked.

"Harry and I named it this morning, when he showed it to me," Garaboxosa said, a smile on his face.

"Tell him its name, Mike," Harry said.

"Snake Eyes," Garaboxosa said. "Look at the barrels."

He set the shotgun on the floor butt-first, and Brad stared at the twin muzzles. They were dark and ominous, like eyes that could kill.

Pendergast picked up something from his desk and walked over to the couch. He knelt down and shook the objects inside his closed fist.

He threw two dice onto the floor.

Brad stared at the white cubes, each with a single dot in the center.

"These are loaded dice from a case we were on some months ago involving some cheating gamblers. The gamblers would palm these and switch dice when a pigeon was winning. They always come up snake eyes."

"Snake eyes means you lose," Garaboxosa said, with obvious glee.

"Snake eyes," Brad said as he picked up the dice, shook them, and rolled them on the floor.

"That's right," Harry said. "Snake eyes means you lose. Every time."

Brad picked up the shotgun and whispered its name again.

The other men in the room smiled in approval.

"Thank you, Harry," Brad said. "It's a fine weapon."

Then Brad slipped Snake Eyes back in its scabbard. He rubbed his fingerprints off the sheath.

"I won't use it for bird hunting," he said. "That's for sure. Not with that double-ought buck."

None of the men said anything as the silence in the room deepened. It was as if a well had been opened in the middle of the office and they were all staring into its dark depths.

FOUR

∾

They rode through a pale dawn, north to LaPorte, where they would cross the South Platte and follow the Cache la Poudre into the formidable mountains. Brad and Mike shivered in their sheep-lined jackets as they left Denver behind, a gray mass of buildings still asleep under a slate sky and a dim sun far to the east, like a lighthouse lamp in fog.

Brad's belly was full after a predawn breakfast at the hotel. Garaboxosa's appetite was astonishing. He had bolted down ham and eggs, biscuits and lumpy mashed potatoes like a condemned man devouring his last meal. Four cups of strong coffee, laced with dissolved sugar, took some of the tiredness out of Brad, but his eyes still ached from the long trek to Denver.

Garaboxosa rode a small horse with small feet, a dun-colored cow pony that he must have bought from the Cheyenne up in Wyoming. The horse couldn't have been more than thirteen or fourteen hands high, and Garaboxosa was a lump of a man in the saddle, a worn cradle of tired and wan leather that seemed more fit for a child than a grown man. His shotgun hung from a D-ring and was strapped to one of the cinches so that it didn't bounce off the horse's hide. On the other side, he carried a battered Henry in an equally worn scabbard that was as thin as rice paper from wear.

"What do you call that little gelding?" Brad asked when Denver was no more than a memory behind them.

"I call him Sparrow," Mike said.

"Sparrow?"

"Because he is small but can fly like a bird. We do not have sparrows in the Pyrenees, so there is no word for that bird in the Basque language."

"Good name," Brad said, and they rode on in silence as the mountains emerged from the darkness of night and the faded blush of dawn. A fresh breeze plied the topknots of the two horses with playful fingers and splashed against their faces like cool, dry water.

"There is a friend waiting for us in LaPorte," Mike said as they passed small ranches and farms, their fields still fallow on the rim of spring, seemingly deserted at that hour of the morning.

"You seem sure of that, Mike," Brad said.

"He will have word of the other herders who are driving their sheep down from Cheyenne."

"Do you expect any trouble on the drive?" Brad asked. "I mean from cattlemen?"

"No. As long as the herders keep the sheep moving, there will be no trouble. The cattlemen are wrong about sheep."

"How are they wrong, Mike?"

"The cattlemen say the sheep ruin the grass. They say that they chew the grass down to the roots and then eat the roots. This is not true. This is why we herd our sheep. We keep them moving so that they do not eat all the grass. We do not just let our sheep graze in one place."

"That's the story, though," Brad said.

"I know. And it is not true. We come to the same places to

graze our sheep year after year and the grass still grows and our sheep grow fat. We have even grazed our sheep where cattle feed and there is no difference. Sheep and cattle eat the same grass and do not fight over territory. Only cattlemen and sheepmen fight over the grasslands."

"That's something to think about," Brad said.

"You do not believe me," Mike said.

"I believe that's what you think. I may have to see it for myself."

"You will see," Mike promised.

The two men spoke but little the rest of the way to LaPorte. They waited on the side of the road when a stage rumbled past from Cheyenne or Fort Collins. They touched their hat brims when they encountered a farmer or a rancher passing them with wagons, full or empty, and they acknowledged strangers heading for Denver. None passed them heading north, however.

Brad was impressed with Mike's pony, Sparrow, who kept up with Ginger and did not seem to tire. They ate as they rode and did not make camp at night but continued on in the darkness along the moonlit road, hearing the chromatic calls of coyotes and watching the bullbats gobble up flying insects after dusk.

Just as Mike had said, there was a sheepman waiting for them in LaPorte. Mike introduced Brad to Belen Agapio.

"You can call me Bill," Agapio said as the two men shook hands.

"All right, Bill."

Then Bill turned to Mike.

"The herds should be coming into the valleys by now," he said. "I saw them leave Cheyenne a week ago."

"Good," Mike said. "I am anxious to see Arramospe."

As the three men crossed the South Platte and headed up Poudre Canyon, Mike explained that Joe Arramospe was a kind of foreman. He managed all the herders and the various flocks that would spend the summer getting fat feeding on mountain grass.

"There will be lambs, soon," he said, "and they will grow strong in the mountains and be ready to make the trip back to Cheyenne with their mothers."

"When will you shear the sheep?" Mike asked.

"They have all been sheared. They will grow their wool back before the trees shed their leaves."

"So they are coming into the high country naked," Brad said.

"As jaybirds," Mike said, with a laugh.

They veered away from the Cache la Poudre after a day and a half of climbing, and in another day they rode into a wide valley nestled among the jagged, snow-capped peaks of the Rockies. Sheep flowed like white water over the hillocks and hillsides. At the far end, Brad saw a number of log cabins. They looked small and cramped and too low for him to stand up in once he was inside. Men were hauling downed pines to a new building site while others barked and notched the logs for a new dwelling.

Joe Arramospe rode out to greet them, his face bathed in sweat. He and Mike spoke to each other in the Basque language before Mike introduced the two men. Joe seemed angry, and while he and Mike spoke, his eyes clenched into tiny fists and tears leaked through the lids and streamed down his face.

Joe had a moon face, darkened from the sun, and his brown eyes rolled around in their sockets like errant marbles as he spoke and gesticulated wildly with his arms and hands.

Mike's and Bill's faces were somber, their expressions drawn taut with an inward sadness.

Brad did not understand one word that Arramospe was saying. When he was finished speaking, Mike turned to Brad.

"We will follow Joe to another valley just beyond this one. He has something to show us."

"Something bad, I gather," Brad said.

"Very bad, very, very bad."

That was all Mike said as he, Bill, and Brad followed Joe
Arramospe to a narrow trail through the timber. Brad noticed
that each of them had the sawed-off shotguns slung to their
saddles and carried rifles, as well. These were rugged men,
he decided, not at all what he imagined sheepherders should
look like. Joe was round-shouldered, but his arms were mus-
cled and his wrists thick, his hands the hands of a working
man, hard and calloused, stained a rich brown by many hours
in the sun.

Before they reached the meadow, Brad heard the faint
bleating of sheep. He also heard the high-pitched staccato
screams of women, a sound that sent shivers up his spine as
if someone had poured icy water on his back.

They emerged from the woods, and Brad saw sheep scattered all over a grassy hillside that butted up against a small
limestone bluff. At the bottom of the bowl-shaped valley,
there were a half dozen log shacks that appeared to have been
hastily thrown together. A clump of women huddled together
in front of one of the huts, their arms around each other, wail-
ing with the trilling sounds he had once heard from Indian
women of the Arapaho tribe. The sound chilled him so that his
arms broke out in goose bumps and there was an icy freshet
coursing up his spine.

To his surprise, Joe led them away from the keening
women and up to one end of the bluffs where there were a
number of juniper trees. He saw something dangling from
one of the trees, something twisting slowly in the slight breeze
that blew down from the high peaks.

As the riders drew closer, Brad saw what was hanging
from the juniper tree.

There, a few yards away, was a man with a rope around
his neck. His head lolled against the upper part of his chest.
His eyes were open and glassy as he stared downward in
sightless death.

The men with Brad crossed themselves and halted their horses. Brad reined up and, while the others stared at the hanged man, scanned the surrounding area, the bald spot above the stand of junipers.

He sensed that something was wrong, that they were not alone. In that clearing, a place where dirt and rocks had run down after rainfall or a heavy snow, there was a thicket of alder and second-growth brush.

"Cut him down," Mike said to Bill and Joe.

"No," Brad said in a loud whisper. "Don't go near that man."

"But that is the body of our friend, Rafael Polentzi. We must bury him."

"Just stay quiet for a minute," Brad said, his voice barely audible.

"Who is this man to tell us what to do?" Joe asked.

"He is a detective," Mike said as he stared at Brad. "I think he is detecting."

The three men looked at Brad, who still stared upward at the thick brush just above the loose dirt and rocks.

There, in the disturbed tailings from a hidden ledge where the brush stood, he saw depressions that could have been left by a man's boots as he climbed up through that soft gravel.

"Turn your horses," Brad said as he dismounted and handed the reins to Mike. "Ride off a little ways, while I take a closer look at something."

Joe opened his mouth to protest, but Mike waved him to silence. He turned his horse, and the others followed.

Brad hunched over and started to walk toward the clump of brush. The other men stopped to watch him.

As he drew close to the small river of dirt, Brad saw some of the brush move. He knew, then, that there was at least one man hiding behind the thick alder. The leaves on the lower branches jiggled slightly while the upper ones ruffled less in the soft breeze.

As the three Basque men watched, Brad reached for the leather thong that hung around his neck. He pulled out a set of rattlesnake rattles. He crouched even lower and shook the rattles.

They all heard it, and the sound startled them.

It startled the man hiding in the brush, too, because he stood up and tried to climb away from the sound. The man was carrying a rifle.

Then the man turned his head and saw Brad hunched over less than thirty yards away. He whirled and started to bring the rifle to his shoulder.

Storm drew his pistol and fired at the man with the rifle.

The rattling stopped, and the explosion from Brad's Colt rumbled along the bluffs and echoed through the trees. Orange flame and lead spewed from the barrel of the pistol.

The man clutched his chest as the .45-caliber bullet smashed into his breastbone, flattened, and ripped a bloody hole in his back. Blood flowered on his chest around a black spot where the bullet had entered. He gasped once and gurgled a choking cry of pain. His rifle dropped from his grasp, and he tumbled forward through the brush and slid down the talus slope in a dead heap.

Brad turned to the sheepmen and held the muzzle of his pistol close to his mouth. He blew away the tassel of smoke that spiraled from the barrel of his Colt. "You can cut your friend down now," he said softly.

He ejected the hull of the expended bullet and slid a fresh one in the cylinder.

None of the Basques moved.

They just stared at Brad in stark astonishment for a long moment as if they were dumbstruck.

The women stopped keening and looked at the man standing alone, on foot, near the dead man dangling at the end of a rope from the juniper tree.

The sheep stopped bleating.

There was a long silence that seemed to last an eternity as the echoes of the gunshot died away to exist only in the shadowy recesses of memory.

FIVE

∽

Brad holstered his pistol and dropped the rattles back inside his shirt.

The silence was broken as the three men rode up to the juniper tree to cut the rope that held their friend.

Brad walked over to the man he had just shot. He turned him over and looked at his face. Then he dragged him by the feet to level ground, squatted over him, and went through his pockets. He pulled out cigarettes, matches, a poker chip, and a wallet with the man's name in it, along with a five-dollar bill.

Mike rode over and looked down at the body.

"He is just a boy," Mike said.

"No more than fifteen or sixteen, looks like," Brad said.

"A pity."

"I don't think he was the one who hanged your friend. This boy had help."

"Maybe so."

"The others may be watching us right now," Brad said. He

looked up at the bluffs and scanned the rimrock. He couldn't be sure, but he thought he saw a glint of light by some rocks atop the sheer escarpment. He stared and stared but saw it no more.

Bill and Joe caught the body of their dead friend, and Bill draped his body across his saddle after he scooted to a spot behind the cantle. The two rode toward the women outside the log huts. Brad mounted his horse. He and Mike joined the solemn procession.

The women pulled at their hair and some scooped up handfuls of dirt and anointed themselves by splashing the dirt onto their heads. Many of them moaned in sorrow and rubbed their reddened eyes or wiped tear streaks from their faces.

One of the women broke free of the others and rushed out to the body on Bill's horse. She screamed when she saw the cut rope around the dead man's neck. She tore at her hair and wailed. Two other women ran out and grabbed the woman and carried her, screaming and kicking, back to their midst where they wrapped her in their arms and stroked her dirt-filled hair.

"That is the widow," Mike said. "Her name is Leda. They have a son who is eight years old."

Brad dismounted and helped carry the dead man into one of the huts. The women had prepared a table, clearing it off and covering it with a blanket. Bill and Brad laid the man gently atop the table, faceup, and then stepped out of the way while Joe slipped the noose from around his neck.

"Let us go outside," Joe said. "Let the women come inside to grieve and wash our friend's body to prepare him for burial."

When they went back outside, five men, ranging in age from eighteen to thirty or so, rushed up and started haranguing Joe in the Basque language. Brad stood aside, trying to look inconspicuous. Mike came over and put an arm on his shoulder. He spoke to the men.

"This is Brad Storm, the man I hired to help us fight the Snake who murdered two of our compatriots. He is a detective. He is the man who just shot one of those cowboys." He turned and pointed to the body on the hillside. "Go and take your anger out on that dead man. Scatter his bones to the wind."

Joe held a sheet of paper in his hand. He handed it to Mike, who read it and handed it to Brad.

"What does that paper say?" one of the men asked.

Brad handed the paper over to Bill.

"Joe found this inside Polentzi's shirt," Mike said, in a loud voice. "It is a warning to all of us."

"What does it say?" asked another man, the oldest in the group.

"It says, 'Get out you filthy sheepherders or you will die.'"

The men grumbled and cursed in loud voices. Their anger showed on their faces. Then the oldest man pulled his knife from its sheath on his belt and held it high in the air. He said something in Basque, then started running toward the man Brad had killed. The others followed, all waving knives in the air, knives that flashed silver bolts in the sun.

A look of sadness came over Mike's face.

"By tomorrow," he said, "the other herders will be here, and these valleys will flow with sheep. I hope you can find this Snake and kill him or take him to Denver to be hanged."

"I'm going to see if I can pick up on the tracks of the men who hanged your friend," Brad said. "I may be gone for a few days."

"Do you wish me to come with you?"

"No. If I need help, I'll ride back and we'll put together some men to go after those killers."

"I am glad you are on our side, Brad."

"I wouldn't have it any other way, Mike."

"Even though we are sheepherders?"

"Mike, when I see an injustice it makes my blood boil. I have had my share of troubles with law breakers. You and your friends have been wronged, brutally wronged. And I've been hired to help you. It will be my pleasure to bring this Schneck and his henchmen to justice."

"What do you mean by justice, Brad?" Mike asked. "Personally or legally?"

"Personally. I think we both know what is meant by 'legally.'"

"Yes," Mike said.

"Personally, justice to me is that the men I'm after will either face the gallows or the grave."

"And, does it make any difference which?"

"I'd like to bring the murderer or murderers before the court in Denver. But if I am unable to do that, I will bring their dead bodies to Boot Hill."

"That is good enough for me, Brad."

"I hope it is good enough for the judge in Denver."

It was then that three women emerged from the cabin. One of them was Leda Polentzi, the widow of Rafael. She, like the other women, wore a multicolored dress, consisting of layers of dyed sackcloth—red, green, black, and yellow. Lace-up boots, a woolen sweater, and a bright orange scarf completed her wardrobe.

"I have just learned that you killed the man who murdered my husband," she said to Storm. "I am very grateful, and I will pray for you."

She reached up and touched his hand. He looked into her hazel eyes. They were brimmed with tears. Her dark hair framed an oval face that was smooth and did not yet show lines of age or furrows of worry on her forehead. Brad figured her to be in her early twenties, although her eyes reflected a wisdom beyond her young years.

"I am sorry for your loss, ma'am," Brad said and patted the back of her hand.

"There is much sorrow here," she said. "Rafael was a good man, a good husband, and the father of our child. I am so sad that he has gone to heaven."

"Yes'm," Brad said, "so am I."

He did not tell her that there were probably more men involved in the hanging than the one he had shot. He just looked at her until she broke their locked gaze and turned and joined the other two women. Together they went back into the gloom of the cabin where her husband lay dead on a table, already stripped of his clothing, naked, awaiting the cleansing of his corpse.

Brad glanced sidelong at the top of the bluff. He saw the tiny flash of light that told him someone was looking down on them with binoculars.

"Don't look at the bluffs, Mike," he said, "but we are being watched. I'm going up there to see if I can flush out the other men who helped with the hanging."

Mike resisted the impulse to look toward the bluffs. He was beginning to trust this quiet man who had given him confidence that the killing would stop.

"I wish you the good luck, Brad," Mike said. "Take care when you go after them."

Brad said nothing. He turned Ginger and rode off toward the far end of the bluffs, where the valley met yet another patch of thick forest. He hoped that the men atop the bluff would think that he was leaving and would continue to lie there in the brush passing a pair of binoculars back and forth. He knew he could ride up to the sloping far end of the ridge and perhaps come upon them before they lit a shuck and left their position.

He felt their eyes on him as he crossed the valley and saw the few head of sheep grazing on the shoots of grass that were pushing up from the soil. He thought of his own cattle streaming into just such a foraging place on his ranch and longed to be home with Felicity in time for the calving that was sure to come.

Brad disappeared into the timber and followed a game trail up the slope, careful to make as little noise as possible. His nostrils filled with the heady scent of pine, spruce, juniper,

and fir. A chipmunk squealed and dashed away ahead of
him, its tail wagging a frantic semaphore until it disappeared
into a hole behind a rock. Blue jays screeched, sending out a
warning to all who would hear, their calls reaching both the
valley and the escarpment in the thin mountain air.

Ginger stepped on earth enriched by the snowmelt and
still soft and damp under the canopy of pines. Brad saw wolf
tracks and cougar tracks and could smell their scents mixed
in with the heady aroma of loam. He reached the top and
wended his way toward the place where he had seen the flash
of sunlight on glass, making a wide semicircle to come up
behind the man or men who lay there, watching the sheep
camp.

The timber thinned, and he avoided the decomposing
deadfalls that were strewn in the underbrush. He felt at home
there, high above the valley, slipping through the tall pines
and past old elk rubs on shattered juniper trees. A hawk floated
in the sky above him and the jays followed, flitting from
branch to branch, oddly silent, as if they had accepted him as
just another denizen of the forest and the mountains. Small
clouds flocked the sky, white against the stark, eye-breaking
blue, and sunlight streamed through the trees and danced
with dust motes that were like ghostly fireflies in the shafts
of pale golden light.

He wondered where the cattle ranchers were grazing their
herd. He wondered how big the herd was and how many men
Schneck had brought with him to the high country. So many
questions, so many doubts.

Now he concentrated on making a beeline for where he
had seen the light. He rode by dead reckoning, sure of his
grasp of terrain and distance. He sniffed the air for the smell
of horses, their droppings, the leather saddles. He trusted his
nose, his sense of smell. In the wilderness, he knew a man
must be always aware of his surroundings, which meant that
he must pay close attention to the feel of the air on his skin,

the scent in his nostrils, and whatever sounds, distant or close, soft or loud, that reached his ears.

A blind man could do no better than Brad when it came to the full use of his senses. The senses were his way of seeing without seeing in the thick timber or out on the prairie.

As he drew closer to the rim of the bluffs, he reined up Ginger and stopped him in his tracks.

He waited long moments and listened for the slightest sound, the wheeze of a horse, the clump of a footfall, the clearing of a man's throat.

He waited and listened with the patience of a hunter, the stalking intensity of a mountain lion.

It was very quiet, but he knew he was close to men who might be waiting in ambush.

For Brad knew that the hunter could also become the hunted.

He sat there on that solemn and silent edge of consciousness where all of his senses were tuned to the highest pitch, waiting for that moment when prey might step out from hiding and stand still for a fraction of eternity, suspicious and wary in the deep and invisible silence.

SIX

❧

Halbert Sweeney handed the binoculars to the man next to him, LouDon Jackson.

"That sure as hell ain't no sheepherder," Sweeney said.

"Did you see how fast that bastard drew his gun?" Jackson said. "No, he ain't no sheepherder."

"I never knowed nobody to slap leather that quick. Poor Rudy never had a chance."

"Why in hell did Rudolph stand up right out there in the open? Like he was scared or somethin'?"

"I don't know, but that was some fancy shootin'. I wish Rudy had ducked or run away."

They watched as Storm went through Rudy's pockets, then saw Storm walk over to talk to the other sheepmen.

The two men continued to observe Storm through the binoculars. Finally, they watched him ride across the valley alone. They only saw a few sheep and one sheepdog with a shepherd tending to the small flock.

"I guess that jasper's leavin', LouDon," Sweeney said.

"Yeah, but where's he goin'?"

"Hell, I don't know. Probably someplace where he don't have to listen to them hysterical women. Did you ever hear such a caterwaulin'?"

"I don't trust that soddy," Sweeney said. "There's somethin' about the way he sits that horse and the way he shot poor Rudy. I'll bet them sheepherders done hired themselves a gunslinger."

"Well, Snake ain't goin' to like it none."

"To hell with Snake. I didn't sign on to rope no boy and string him up."

"Otto wants them sheep out of the valley," Sweeney said.

"Hell, there ain't enough sheep to make a stew," LouDon said.

"I don't see what's got Schneck in such a dither, then. Unless they's more sheep on the way."

"That's probably it, Hal. Snake don't want no sheep goblin' up all the grass up here."

The two men continued to watch as Brad disappeared into the timber. They looked down at the sheepherders for a few minutes, and then LouDon took off the binoculars and put them back in their case.

Both men crawled backward away from the rim of the bluffs. They stood up and started to walk toward their horses, which were ground-tied to a pine some yards away.

As they neared their mounts, Sweeney halted suddenly and put out a hand to stay LouDon.

"Listen," he said. "I thought I heard somethin'. Off yonder." He pointed to the thick woods beyond where they stood.

"Yeah. I think that gunslick must've rid up here to get after us. They's somebody out there, sure as hell."

"Let's get out of here," Sweeney said in a loud whisper.

The two men tiptoed to their horses, untied the reins, and stepped into their saddles.

They had begun to ride away when Storm stepped into view. He was on foot and held a Winchester rifle in his hands.

There was no time to think.

The two men put spurs to their horses and galloped away. They disappeared into the deep timber, turning their horses to race away in a zigzag pattern. They both looked back, expecting to hear a rifle shot at any time.

"We lost him," Sweeney said, panting for breath.

"Yeah, but for how long?" LouDon said. "That sonofabitch is like a burr under the saddle. We ain't never goin' to get rid of him."

"Snake will know what to do."

LouDon fixed Hal with a hard accusing stare.

"We ain't goin' to tell Snake how close we come to gettin' our lamps put out, Hal. You got that?"

"I got it. But we got to tell him about the gunslick, what he done to Rudy."

"Yeah, but that's all, hear?"

"Okay, LouDon. We'll just tell him about that jasper shootin' Rudy."

The two men rode for the high ridge that bordered another valley where the Schneck herd of cattle fed on shoots of grass an inch high. The men's stomachs were in knots, and if they hadn't had their reins and saddle horns to hold on to as they rode, their hands would have been trembling.

They were both afraid of that lone man they had seen standing less than a hundred yards away with a rifle in his hands.

They did not know his name or who he was, but they knew one thing: The gunslinger who had shot Rudy dead was a dangerous man.

SEVEN

∾

Brad watched the two men run to their horses and ride away into the heavy timber. He got a good look at them. One was tall and wore a battered brown hat, a red neckerchief, a heavy duck jacket with some kind of winter lining, and brown and yellow boots. The other, six inches shorter, wore a gray hat that had all but lost its blocked shape, sporting a leather band. He wore a faded blue neckerchief. He had heavy features, a large nose, and bulbous cheeks that echoed his fat, round torso. He wore faded denim trousers and a moth-eaten leather jacket with a sheepskin collar. The taller man appeared to have light sandy hair, chiseled cheekbones, and a hooked nose that protruded over a light blond moustache as bushy as the bristles on a shaving brush.

Both men rode heavy-boned geldings with dark tan hides and big feet and black manes. Their saddles might have come from Cheyenne or Denver—not fancy, but well worn, with coiled lariats hooked to D-rings near the pommel. Easy to reach for a working cowhand, Brad thought.

"Well, boys," he said to himself, "you sure as hell left some mighty fine tracks."

He walked back to where he had ground-tied Ginger, shoved the Winchester back in its boot, and climbed into the saddle. As he was riding toward the spot where the two men had tethered their horses, he heard a soft whicker from another direction. He pinpointed the location when the horse snorted and heard the sound of its hooves pawing the ground.

He approached cautiously, his right hand at rest on the butt of his pistol. The horse nickered and Ginger answered. Brad held his horse to a slow walk and approached a dun horse standing next to a pine tree surrounded by small firs and spruces. He waited a few minutes, listening for any other sounds, then rode up to the horse. He assumed that it belonged to the man he had shot and killed. The brand on its hip was a wavy Slash S.

He rode up and opened a flap on the left saddlebag. There was a plug of chewing tobacco, a box of .30-caliber Sharps cartridges, a sack of smoking tobacco, a box of wooden matches, and a packet of rolling papers. He looked in the other saddlebag and saw the remnants of a beef sandwich, the meat slathered with mustard and sprinkled with black peppers. It was wrapped in thin oil paper. There was a small bottle of cheap whiskey that was half full and a box of hard candies that were all stuck together. A wooden canteen hung from the saddle horn, and the empty boot testified that the man who had owned the horse was the man waiting in the bushes with the single-shot Sharps rifle.

Sad, he thought, that a young man's life was cut so short. Even sadder to find his horse and know that the dead man had ridden it over many trails and would never ride again. In another time and place, the dead man might have been an upstanding citizen, a law-abiding cowhand who lived by the Code of the West. Instead, he had been ordered to step beyond his line of work because of another man's merciless greed. When you worked for Schneck, he surmised, you weren't just

riding for the brand, you were carrying out murderous orders
that had nothing to do with the cattle business.

Brad felt his anger rising as he looked at the forlorn dun,
standing there hipshot, deprived of his owner and rider. He
vowed, upon his return, to take the horse to Bill if he had use
for it, and if not, perhaps he would add the animal to his own
remuda when he returned home.

He followed the tracks of the dun horse and hoped they
would join up with the other two horses ridden by the men
with the binoculars. It was slow tracking through the scattered pine needles and rotting cones, but he was experienced
and knew what signs to look for, signs that would mark a
horse's passing over all but solid rock.

The tracks of the dun did converge with the tracks of the
other two horses who had laid footprints in two directions. He
was pleased to find that all three men had followed a game
trail. A little farther on, he found another track and a fresh
blaze on a pine tree. He was tempted to follow those tracks,
since they continued on toward the valley where the sheepmen and their families were quartered. But he decided against
it for the time being. He vowed to return to that blaze and
follow the one-way tracks, since he had a strong hunch where
they would lead.

Brad figured that Schneck had sent a lone scout to find out
where the sheepherders were. Then that man had circled back
and left a blazed trail for the three men who returned to rope
and hang Polentzi as a warning.

The question in Brad's mind was when had the bark been
chopped away to leave a blaze mark on that tree? Was it on
the way to the bluff and the valley or on the way back? He
circled the tracks and deciphered their meaning after a few
minutes of scrutiny. He looked again at the pine tree and saw
that it was standing alone in a small clearing, easily seen by
anyone riding along the well-worn game trail. The scout's
tracks went both ways, at a different angle from the others
and from the trail. So, the scout had probably found the

sheepmen either as they entered the valley or shortly after their arrival, then had returned to hack that blaze on the pine tree. Further examination of the tracks revealed that the scout had cut a low-hanging branch from another pine tree and used it as a trailing broom to erase his tracks off the trail.

So, Brad figured, the scout had returned to his cow camp by a different route, and he didn't want others following that course.

Brad wondered who the scout was. He was obviously an experienced tracker and perhaps a woodsman. He had taken some pains to wipe out his horse's hoofprints and may have spent a day or two, or longer, scouting the valley before he returned and used a small hatchet to strike that fresh scar in the pine tree.

Brad continued to follow the tracks of the two men who had been observers atop the rimrock. Along the trail, he found other blazes, close together, and tracks of the scout's horse, heading in the same direction, with no attempt to blot them out. So, he surmised that the scout had circled back to the game trail and marked the path for those who were to follow him and find the sheep camp.

So now he was following three sets of tracks heading back to the cow camp with the dun tracks going along only one way.

He rode into thick timber with several rocky outcroppings that rose up from the underbrush like ancient stone idols in ruin. He also saw elk and mule deer tracks, and, in one place, came across a shallow wallow where elk had bedded down a few days before. Their scent was thick in the air, and he saw hairs from their hides stuck to the pines and junipers. He rounded old deadfalls of huge trees that the bears had plumbed for grubs and that nature's rains and snows had penetrated to render the trunks into dust and pulp.

The land began to slope upward and soon Ginger was climbing. Brad sensed that he was nearing a dramatic change in terrain, perhaps a ridge overlooking another big valley where cattle could graze. There were more elk and deer tracks, crisscrossing the wending game trail and other such trails branching off that one.

He stopped often during the slow climb up the sloping land, to listen and to look around him. He saw another blazed tree near the top of the slope and headed toward it. Horse tracks overlaid the game tracks in the soft wet soil, and there were horse hairs clinging to the bark of pine trees where the horses had rubbed against the scaly trunks.

It was eerie in that realm of the forest with tall pines standing thick, their canopies high above the earth, the needles bristling with sunlight that dappled the ground where it leaked through and played with shadows. It was very quiet until he reached level ground atop the slope.

That's when he heard the distant sound of cattle bawling and knew that he was nearing the grazing grounds. He spoke in soft tones to Ginger, telling him to be quiet and not let out a whinny, in case there were horses nearby. He topped the slope and felt that he was atop a long wide ridge that divided the timber from the open range beyond. He saw craggy, snow-capped mountains in the distance, purple and hazy ridges in between him and the majestic peaks, standing there like frozen ocean waves, one after the other rising and falling, seemingly endless.

He rode to the center of the ridge and then stopped short at the sound of an ax ringing on a tree. He heard a horse neigh off to his left from a place he could not see. As he listened, he heard the sound of a saw cutting through wood in counterpoint to the ring of the ax biting into a pine trunk.

Wary, Brad angled toward the sounds. He caught a glimpse of a wood cart hitched to a mule and horses standing ground-tied to brush well past the cart. He edged toward the far side of the ridge and, in the concealment of a pair of blue spruces, he peered down into a huge valley already greening up with spring grass. He saw white-faced cattle grazing along a creek and the tiny shapes of men on horseback driving more cattle into the valley and herding them onto different parts of the grassland.

There was a spiral of grayish blue smoke rising through the trees at the far end of the valley, and he caught a glimpse of a log structure there, hand-hewn benches around a large fire ring. Nearby, there stood a chuck wagon and an aproned man tending to the open fire, his kettles and irons set over and around the fire.

Horses, unsaddled, stood under a large lean-to surrounded by pines with a large hay wagon parked near it, its tongue touching the ground, its racks askew around an empty bed.

Suddenly, the sounds of the ax and the saw stopped and the silence seemed deafening.

Brad turned Ginger to cross back over the wide ridge.

That's when he heard the snap-click of a lever on a rifle as a shell was jacked into the firing chamber.

He turned his head and saw three men standing less than a hundred yards away. One of them held a rifle, one an ax, and the other had a pistol in his hand.

"Mister, you drop that gun belt and step down from that horse or I'll drop you like a lump of shit down a privy," the man with the rifle said.

To emphasize his threat, the man raised his rifle to his shoulder and lined up the front and rear sights.

Brad froze in the saddle.

There was no place to run, no place to hide.

EIGHT

∾

Brad let both hands drop slowly to his belt buckle. He moved his fingers, but made no move to slip the belt out of the buckle.

The three men began to walk toward him. The man with the rifle eased the stock down from his shoulder. The man with the ax carried it as a soldier would hold a rifle, across his chest, while the man with the pistol in his hand tilted it so that the barrel pointed downward.

Brad's brain circuits ignited like streaks of lightning. Thoughts stormed through his mind with the speed of a prairie whirlwind.

Three men on foot. He on a horse. Who was the dominant figure here? He had speed and mobility. The three men had neither. They were armed, but so was he.

And Brad knew a trick or two for just such a situation.

There was only one thing to do or he was a dead man.

Brad dug his spurs into Ginger's flanks and ducked low on the saddle. He slid to the right side of his horse and drew his six-gun, all in one fluid motion. He drew a bead on the man with the rifle, cocked his pistol, and squeezed the trigger. He hugged the side of his horse, Indian style, the way he had seen Arapaho braves play at war on their barebacked ponies.

Ginger charged straight at the three men, and Brad's shot zizzed over the rifleman's head. The rifleman threw himself to one side, his face drained of blood. The man with the ax stumbled backward to avoid the charging horse, while the man with the pistol jumped to his left and fell into the man with the rifle.

Brad turned Ginger slightly to his left and fired off two more quick shots. Dirt spurted up between the three men as Brad's bullets plowed furrows in the soft damp soil, kicking up dust and sand, injecting fear in the three men who now sprawled facedown, their weapons as useless as children's play toys.

Brad heeled Ginger over in a tight turn and galloped past the three men on the ground. He passed the wood cart and flew into the timber, Ginger's mane and tail streaming in the breeze like guidon pennants in a downhill cavalry charge. He did not stop but let his horse weave the way through the pines and dodge the firs, spruce, and junipers like a slalom racer on a ski slope.

Brad heard the men shouting at him.

"You bastard," one of them yelled.

"Come back, you coward, and fight like a man," another hollered.

"Who in hell was that?" screeched another in a high-pitched voice.

He slowed Ginger to a walk and circled back to the game trail he had followed to the ridgetop.

Now he knew where the cow camp was, and that was enough for the time being. He would have to return and scout the adjoining timber and figure out how to capture or kill

Otto Schneck. It would not be an easy task. Schneck's men would be on their guard now. At least five of his men had seen him and knew what he looked like and what kind of horse he rode.

But he had some advantage, he figured. They would not know where he was when he came back and would not even know that he was nearby. He would be a shadow in the timber, a lone wolf prowling the perimeter of the valley, watching, waiting, and listening. Already, plans were forming in his mind. And he knew that his goal was to find Schneck, catch him unaware, and complete his assignment. Then he could return home and resign his job as a private detective. That would please Felicity and him.

He rode on, riding around deadfalls and clumps of brush, passing stone outcroppings with moss growing gray and green on the boulders nearest the ground.

Then he heard an odd sound. At first he thought it might be a squirrel or a chipmunk, gnawing on a tree trunk. Then he heard other sounds that were more familiar, the whack of a hatchet on pine bark. He approached the source of the sounds with caution.

He made sure that Ginger avoided rocks or anything that would announce his presence. He halted the horse when he got very near. More scraping sounds and more whacks from a small hatchet.

He waited and leaned from one side to the other until he spotted the rump of a horse. Then he saw a man in the saddle of that horse, a tall steeldust gray. He watched the man for several seconds.

Then he looked at the trees in the man's wake. The pines were of different sizes and thicknesses. Some had odd marks on them, slashes and small blazes. The man had a knife in one hand and a hatchet in the other. He cut two slanted slashes on some of the trees, and a small square blaze on others, head high.

Brad prodded Ginger forward until he was within a few feet of the man on the steeldust.

The rider was so intent on his work that he had not heard Brad ride up behind him.

"Howdy," Brad said in his friendliest voice. "What are you doing?"

The man whirled around in the saddle and stared at Brad. He bore no expression on his face.

The man was tall with a shock of light blond hair protruding from beneath his hat. He had a rifle slung from his saddle, and there was a pistol dangling from his gun belt. He had piercing blue eyes, square shoulders, and arms that bulged with muscles under his shirt.

"Marking trees," the man said, "if it's any of your business."

"I was just out hunting and heard you making noise, so rode up to see what you were doing, that's all."

"I'm marking some of the trees for building log cabins and knifing those that can be cut down for firewood. I'm with the wavy Slash S outfit down in the valley."

Brad looked downward at the steeldust's tracks.

He had found the scout who had blazed the trail to the sheep camp.

"I thought I heard shots," the man said. "Was that you?"

"A cow elk. I missed her."

"Sounded like you was mighty close to where our cattle camp is."

The man had a slight accent. Swedish or Danish, Brad figured.

"Well, I didn't see any cows. Just the cow elk."

"What's your handle?" the man asked.

"Brad. Brad Storm. Yours?"

"I'm Thorvald Sorenson. My friends call me Thor."

"Swedish?"

"I'm a Swede, *jah*, from Minnesota. I was a logger up there and come west. A cattleman hired me up in Cheyenne.

I do some scoutin' for him and, since I know timber, I mark the trees for the woodcutters."

"I raise cattle myself," Brad said.

"Oh? You live hereabouts?"

Brad sensed that he might make a friend out of Sorenson, even though that friendship might be very brief, so he did not want to make the man suspicious or be caught in a bald-faced lie.

"Over to Leadville, if you know where that is. West of Denver."

"Never heard of it."

"It's a little mining town, but there is good graze for cattle in the summer months. I have a small ranch there."

"You might want to meet my boss, then. Otto Schneck, a German. You and him have a lot in common."

"Maybe when I get my elk," Brad said.

"Where you camped?" Sorenson asked.

Brad stiffened inwardly. The man knew where the sheep-herders were camped and he knew something of the terrain in this part of the country.

"Way down on the Poudre," Brad said. "I do some fishing for trout when I'm not out hunting."

"I know the Poudre," Sorenson said. "It's runnin' mighty fast about now."

"Yeah, and it'll get faster." Brad touched a finger to the brim of his hat. "Well, I'm off and wish you luck in marking all those trees."

"You stop by and I'll introduce you to my boss. They call him Snake because of his name, I think. We're in a valley on the yonder end of this ridge."

"I'll do that," Brad said. "I'd like to meet Snake."

Sorenson laughed. It was a wry laugh, as if the two were in some private joke. He raised his knife hand and touched the brim of his hat. He smiled.

Brad turned his horse and rode off through small gullies and rocky outcroppings, his heart hammering in his chest. He kept looking back to see if Sorenson might be following him, but he heard the distant sound of the hatchet cutting into pine bark and knew that the Swede was back to marking trees.

Sooner or later, the man he had just met would find out who he was, that he had shot one of Schneck's men and had a run-in with the ones gathering firewood.

He wondered what Sorenson would think when he knew that Brad was allied with the sheepherders. Was he loyal to Schneck, neutral, or a hireling who might be turned against Schneck?

It was sad to think that he and Sorenson might have to face each other in combat. In another time or place, they might have become good friends. The Swede wasn't a cattleman. He was a woodsman caught up in a brutal range war in which he probably had little or no interest.

He hoped Sorenson would think kindly of him when he found out that he was not camped on the Poudre and he wasn't hunting elk.

But that was probably too much to hope for. If he was working for Schneck, he was one of Schneck's men and he would follow the cattleman's orders.

Brad knew how dangerous it was once the battle lines were drawn.

Here, high in the mountains, where sheepmen and cattlemen fought over the best grass and hated each other, there was only one certainty.

From now on, it was kill or be killed.

Brad was right in the middle of it.

And so was Sorenson.

NINE

∾

The dun horse was still standing where Brad had last seen it. The horse whinnied when he approached and tossed its head in greeting. Ginger nickered softly in reply.

Brad untied the reins. He patted the horse's neck and rubbed it as he spoke to the animal in soothing tones. He looked at its teeth, figuring it to be no more than three or four years old. It had been well cared for. It wore fairly new shoes, and there were signs that its mane and tail had been brushed and its hide curried. Brad pulled on the reins and led the horse back along the path he had taken to reach the top of the ridge. When he emerged from the timber, he saw a cottony clump of sheep being herded by a furry black-and-white dog. A herder with a staff followed on foot. The man waved to Brad and he waved back.

He saw men lowering the body of the man he had shot into a pit at the edge of the tree line below the talus-strewn slope of the lower bluff. Two of the men were smoking pipes, and a man who leaned on a shovel puffed on a hand-rolled cigarette.

Brad rode toward the lean-to that housed the horses and mules. Some of the women eyed him from the doorway of the cabin where he assumed they were dressing the corpse of Polentzi for burial. None of them waved to him.

Inside the lean-to, he unsaddled the two horses and laid the saddles next to a log pole that served as a brace for the bottom of the structure. He draped the blankets and saddlebags over the pole and dipped some grain from a barrel which he poured into a pair of small troughs where he had tethered the dun and Ginger. Having removed a small can of oil and a cleaning rod from his saddlebags, he carried his rifle and shotgun outside, found a log to sit on, and leaned his long weapons against a pine tree. He opened the cloth wrapping and slid his pistol from its holster, ejected the two empty shells from his Colt and the four unfired cartridges. He began to clean his pistol, plumbing the barrel with a wiry brush, then putting a thin film of oil inside the barrel and on the grip, barrel, and cylinder. He drove another brush, a soft one, up and down the inside of the barrel and then wiped the gun clean, leaving a slight patina of oil on all the exposed metal and staghorn grips. He pushed six cartridges into the cylinder, spun it once, then let the hammer fall on a spot between two cylinders so that the hammer would not be touching a firing cap. He holstered his pistol as Mike walked up to him, a pipe clenched between his teeth.

His pipe smoke smelled of apples and moist tobacco. He sat down on the log next to Brad.

"One man buried, another to go," Mike said.

"Senseless," Brad said.

"Yes, but that is what most of life is, senseless."

"Hanging a man does not solve any problems. Neither does killing the man who had a hand in the hanging."

"No," Mike said, "but it does bring matters to a head, does it not?"

"Maybe."

"What did you find on your ride besides the dead man's horse?" Mike asked.

"I found the cattle camp, and I met the scout who led the three men here. I think all three of them roped and hanged your friend Polentzi."

"And did you kill the other two?" Mike let smoke stream from the corners of his mouth and in twin streams through his nose.

"No. I did not see them again. They were the ones who were watching us from the top of that bluff."

"Ah. But you will recognize them when you see them again."

"Probably."

"And you will kill them? When you see them again, I mean."

"If they attack me, maybe. I will not hunt them down just to kill them."

"Why not?"

"They were just following orders. I am after the man who sent them to kill Polentzi."

"They are equally guilty," Mike said.

"Yes, I suppose they are. But to just kill them would not be true or full justice for Polentzi's death."

"Rafael was my brother-in-law," Mike said. "Leda is my blood sister."

Brad reared back in surprise.

"Are all these men and women related to you, Mike?" he asked.

Mike chuckled.

"Many are, but not all. The Basque are few in number, and we seldom marry outside of our own group of countrymen and women."

"Are you married, Mike?"

Mike shook his head. "No. I was married, but my wife died in childbirth after we arrived in Wyoming."

"Will you marry again?"

Mike laughed as if chewing on that bit of irony.

"Ah, if the Fates so decide, perhaps. But I have not seen that glow in a woman's cheeks, nor the flash in her eyes when I come near. As I said, we are few, not only in Europe, in Spain, but here in this country. And we Basques don't really have a country of our own. We don't really have a nationality. We're like orphans of the world."

Smoke entered Brad's nostrils, and he sneezed into his cupped hands.

"Bless you," Mike said.

"That tobacco must have a bite to it, Mike."

"It's Virginia grown. Bought it in Denver."

"Well, maybe it's got some Virginia dust in it."

Mike laughed.

"When's the funeral for your brother-in-law?" Brad asked.

"Probably early in the morning. At sunrise. We'll have our hands full when all those sheep get here. I expect they'll be streaming in here all day and into the night."

"Quite a big herd, then."

"Yes, and we'll graze some of them in that other valley. Bill and I may have to find new pasture for them."

"Which means?"

"We may have to look beyond those bluffs and see what's higher up."

Brad looked up at the bluffs.

"That's where Schneck is grazing his cattle."

"I know. But we have grazed there before Schneck came barging in. It's just below eleven thousand feet, and you'll see our trails all over the place."

"I didn't see any when I rode up there."

"A sheep trail is not very wide. And, after we leave, the deer and elk use the same trails."

"Maybe I did see your trails, or one of them."

"And you saw grass growing, too, didn't you?"

Brad nodded.

"So, you see, we do not ruin pasture. We keep the sheep

moving, and they leave their droppings on the ground, which feeds the grass and keeps the roots warm in winter."

"Cattle do the same."

"Too bad cattle and sheep can't live together in such a beautiful country," Mike said.

"As long as there is prejudice among cattlemen toward sheep, you'll never see cattle and sheep grazing together."

"And that's a shame," Mike said.

"Which reminds me," Brad said, "I did meet and talk to one of the men who works for Schneck. I don't believe he's one of the killers."

"How do you know? How can you be sure?"

"He's not a cattleman. He's not a drover nor a wrangler, either."

"What is he?" Mike asked.

"He's a woodsman, from up north. I think he works as a scout for Schneck."

"A scout?"

"I think he might have been the man who found that valley where Schneck's cattle are grazing. I think he also found this valley and probably told his boss about it. Maybe before you got here."

"Or after," Mike said, a rueful half smile curving his lips.

"That's a possibility. His name is Thorvald Sorenson. He's a Swede. He didn't know who I was, of course. He thinks I'm up here hunting elk."

"You are hunting, all right," Mike said. "But two-legged animals. Because that's what they are those cattlemen—animals."

"I think it's just Schneck who's the animal," Brad said. "He is the one who gives the orders."

"But his men carry them out."

"That doesn't mean his men like the orders he's giving them."

"Maybe you are too tolerant for this job," Mike said, and Brad sensed a testiness in his tone.

"I'm not tolerant of murderers, Mike."

"But Schneck may not have killed my cousin or my brother-in-law. Those murders took more than one man."

"I agree. The men who carried out those orders are equally guilty under the law. I am not absolving them of blame. But they are the body of the snake. It's my job, as I see it, to cut off the head of that snake. And from all indications, that is Schneck."

"What about the men who did the actual killing?"

Brad took in a deep breath.

Mike had asked an important question. It was a question he could not answer just then. He thought he knew what Garaboxosa wanted to hear, but he would not give him that satisfaction. Not yet.

If he were to go after the killers who worked for Schneck, he would need help. Armed help. And that would mean a full-blown range war between cattlemen and sheep ranchers. Such a war might become a western tragedy, involving townspeople, lawmen, and even, perhaps, the military. He didn't want that, and he was sure Pendergast would not want him to carry that much power in his weapons or use that much force.

No, he would not start such a war. He had his assignment and Mike knew damned well what it was. Find the man who ordered the murders and bring him to justice.

Or kill him.

And that was assignment enough for any one man, Brad knew.

He might not be able to exact a pound of flesh from those men who obeyed Schneck's orders, but he had a hunch that he would not have to look for trouble.

Experience had taught him that.

No, he would not have to seek out trouble.

Trouble would find him.

TEN

∽

Otto Schneck was a stalwart man, bullnecked, heavy-shouldered, stocky as a Hereford bull, with orange hair, a brushy blondish moustache threaded with rust, and a mouth as pudgy as a blowfish's. He wore leather straps on each thick wrist, and a wide gun belt draped his ample waist. His pistol nestled in a tie-down holster that was made of woven leather that matched his kangaroo boots. His large hooked nose emphasized the jutted jaw, the high chiseled cheekbones. His eyes were a pale blue that was almost colorless, giving him a vacant expression that was chilling.

He sat at the rustic table listening to the account of the two men who had helped hang the sheepherder. Halbert Sweeney and LouDon Jackson were both from the panhandle of Texas, both bowlegged as pairs of parentheses and balding under their ten-gallon hats. They called Sweeney "Hal" because he didn't like "Bert," and they called Jackson "LouDon," making it into a single word.

Outside were the sounds of cattle and of men chopping wood up on the ridge. Otto could hear the groaning of the wheels on the wood cart as it rumbled onto the flat, and somewhere a horse neighed an arpeggioed ribbon of nasal and throat sounds.

"Sit down," Schneck commanded. Both were standing at one end of the long table having just entered the log cabin to report to their boss. "Where is Rudolph?"

"Rudy's dead, Snake." Hal fished a cheroot from his shirt pocket and bit off the end.

"Dead?"

"Yes, sir, one of them sheepherders shot him plumb dead," Hal said.

"Only I don't think it was no sheepherder," LouDon said.

Schneck fixed Jackson with those cold pale eyes of his.

"What was he, then?"

"He's faster'n greased lightnin', Snake," LouDon said. "He looked more like a damned gunfighter than a sheeper. Rudy never had no chance."

"That right, Hal?" Schneck said, turning his attention to Sweeney.

"They was a bunch of them sheepmen ridin' to where we hanged that Messican kid and this one jasper got off his horse and walk toward where Rudy was hidin' in the bushes. Rudy stood up and went to shoot the man, but he didn't have no chance. No chance at all."

"Why in hell did Rudolph stand up? If he was hiding in the brush, he should have stayed there," Schneck said, his neck pulsating and bulging like a bull in heat. He looked over at Jackson.

"The man did somethin'," LouDon said. "He pulled somethin' from inside his shirt. I couldn't see what it was, but Rudy jumped up like he was scared and started down the hill like somethin' was chasin' him."

"I think there was somethin' in that brush," Hal said.

"Somethin' sure as hell put fire to Rudy's feet. He boiled out of there like somethin' was bitin' him on the ass."

Jackson struck a match and lit Hal's cheroot.

Schneck waved the cloudlet of smoke away after it spewed out of Hal's mouth.

"We heard somethin', I think," Jackson said. "I mean it was far off and hard to hear, but we might have heard it."

Sweeney gave Jackson a dirty look that Schneck could not fail to miss.

"Did you hear something or did you not hear something?" Schneck asked. He looked straight at Sweeney when he said it.

"It all happened so fast, Snake," Sweeney said. "I mean one minute that tall drink of water was walkin' toward the hill where Rudy was hidin' and ready to pick him off a sheepherder or two when they cut down the man we hanged. Rudy never had no chance. One minute the man was just standin' there and the next he had a pistol in his hand. He plugged Rudy with one shot and Rudy fell down dead."

"Rudolph Grunewald was a favorite of mine. He was turning out to be a mighty fine cowhand."

"Yes, sir," Hal said. "I'm real sorry Rudy got kilt."

"I don't know, Snake," Jackson said, blurting the words out. "I heard maybe a buzzin' sound. Coulda been a rattler in them bushes."

"A rattler? This time of year? It's a little early, I think," Schneck said.

"Maybe Rudy woke this'n up," Jackson said lamely.

"I didn't hear no rattler," Hal said, a little too belligerently to suit either Jackson or Schneck.

One of the woodcutters came into the cabin just then. Schneck looked up at him.

"I got somethin' to report, Boss," Cass O'Malley said. "Did you hear them shots up on the ridge a while back?"

"I did. What were you shooting at, snakes?"

"No, sir, weren't us shootin'. It was us getting shot at."

"Maybe you'd better sit down, Cass," Schneck said. "Might as well listen to another tall tale. This seems to be the day for it."

Cass sat down, a puzzled expression on his face.

A horse galloped up near the cabin, and they all heard the creak of leather as a man dismounted.

Then it was quiet. Schneck looked toward the open doorway as if expecting someone to walk through it. But he only heard the sound of the horse pawing the ground outside.

Cass told about the stranger riding up, and how he and Percy Wibble and Ned Kingman challenged the rider.

"We had him braced, Snake," Cass said. "Ned told him to drop his gun belt, and he looked like he was a-goin' to do it, then he up and slid sideways off'n his saddle, drew his pistol faster'n you could say 'Jack Robinson,' and come plumb at us, a-shootin' that six-gun square at us. Well, sir, we all splayed out on the ground and he rode right on past us. Scared me plumb out of my wits. Them bullets plowed the ground right next to me and Percy."

Cass wiped sweat from his forehead with a swipe of his sleeve. He was plainly rattled.

"Did you try and shoot him when he rode on past?" Schneck asked.

"Nope. I was pissin' my pants as it was, Snake. I mean, I thought that man was part Injun or somethin', the way he flattened out aside his big old horse and come at us with his pistol spittin' fire and lead flyin' all around."

"Would you say that this man could have shot you dead, Cass?" Schneck asked.

"Hell, I don't know. It all happened so fast. I didn't even see him draw his gun. We never expected him to come right at us like that."

Schneck looked at Hal and LouDon.

"Sound familiar, boys?" Schneck asked.

Jackson and Sweeney looked at each other.

"Was he a tall man wearin' a Stetson and ridin a strawberry roan with a white blaze on its forehead?" Hal asked.

"Yep. It sure was a man on a strawberry roan."

"Same man," LouDon said.

Just then, Thor Sorenson stepped inside the cabin. He had
been standing outside listening to Cass tell his story.

"Thor, did you hear all that?" Schneck asked. "You were
standing right outside."

"Horse had a splinter under its hoof. I didn't hear anything," Sorenson lied.

"I wonder if you saw a waddie riding a strawberry roan,"
Schneck said.

Sorenson shook his head.

"Did you hear him shootin' at us?" Cass asked.

"Nope," Sorenson said. "I have been making the marks on
the trees for you fellers."

Schneck stared at Sorenson. He wondered if the man was
lying, and if he was lying, why?

Sorenson stood there with no telltale expression on his
face. In fact, he bore no expression whatsoever. He just stood
there as if daring anyone in the room to challenge him. Hal
puffed on his cheroot and dropped the ashes on the dirt floor
of the cabin.

"Sit down, Sorenson," Schneck said. "Cookie's makin'
coffee, and he will bring the pot in here directly."

Sorenson sat down on one of the benches next to the table.
He took off his hat and reshaped the crown as if to show his
disinterest.

Schneck looked at him for a long time before he spoke to
the Swede.

"Well, Thor," he said, finally, "that nobody you didn't see
killed Rudy Grunewald today. Killed him with one shot. And
he shot some bullets at Cass here and just disappeared, I
reckon."

Sorenson looked up at Schneck with that same blank expression on his face.

"It appears to me you got a handful of trouble, Mr. Schneck. I hired on as a scout. Whatever score you have to settle with those sheepherders is betwixt you and them. I ain't rightly no part of it."

"In this outfit, Sorenson, it's one for all and all for one. You got that?"

"There's other jobs," Sorenson said. He put his hat back on and squared it.

"Not as good as this one," Schneck retorted.

"Maybe better," Sorenson said.

"Is that a threat, Sorenson?"

"Nope. I just don't cotton to no gunplay, that's all. Without good reason, anyways."

"You liked Rudolph, didn't you?"

"I thought he was a good kid. Light on brains, but a hard worker."

Schneck stiffened in his chair at the head of the table.

"Well, with this jasper on the roan, we got us a black boy in the woodpile, Sorenson. I want to know if you might be interested in a little bonus, some sugar in your pay."

"That depends, Snake. What kind of string is tied to that bonus?"

"You're a tracker. I want you to track that man down and kill him. His horse tracks should still be fresh."

Sorenson drew in a deep breath.

"Just like that, eh?" he said. "Track a man down and put his lamp out. No judge, no jury, just the law of the six-gun."

"Just like that," Schneck said.

"Otherwise?"

"Otherwise, draw your pay and light a shuck out of here," Schneck said.

Sorenson stood up. He looked at the three other men, then at Schneck.

"I'll sleep on it," he said, and walked out of the cabin. They heard him climb into the saddle and ride away.

"What do you think of that, Snake?" Hal asked. He stubbed

out the butt of his cheroot with his foot, grinding it down into the black earth.

"I think we got more than one darkie in the woodpile," Schneck said, and his cold eyes turned even colder and pale as shirred egg whites in a black bowl.

The three men looked down at their hands as if they wished they were anyplace else but there in that log cabin with Schneck.

None said a word, and Schneck looked at them with contempt as his neck swelled again and turned the color of an April sunset when the sky in the west was on fire.

ELEVEN

&

Mike bunked Brad in a small pitched-roof log dwelling. Brad laid his bedroll out on the dirt floor against the back wall. Joe Arramospe set his blankets at a right angle, with small spruce boughs between him and the floor.

Sitting outside, the two men watched the sky change colors at sunset. They sat on a pair of pine logs sawed in half. Joe smoked a clay pipe with a long stem while the cook prepared stew for supper. The cook, Renata Tiribio, was a sturdy woman married to one of the sheepmen, Nestor, who was driving the flock down from Cheyenne the next morning. Two women brought bowls of the stew over to Joe and Brad, their faces partially hidden by their ample shawls that they wore like cowls. Brad knew they were not young, and their brown faces were lined with the evidence of past sorrows. He and Joe ate from the steaming bowls and washed down the food from canteens filled with cold creek water. The western sky became a bright smear of red streamers tinged with gold and the ashes of clouds floating in a netherworld of pale blue sky and encroaching dusk.

Mike walked over after supper and squatted in front of the two men, a pipe clenched in his teeth.

"There will be coffee," he said. "Weak coffee so that we will all be able to sleep. Vivelda will bring us our cups."

"I will patrol the pasture," Joe said, "until midnight, when Fidelio will relieve me."

Mike turned to look at Brad.

"Fidelio Yorick is Joe's cousin," he said to Brad. "He is also the brother-in-law of the man who was killed and be-headed. His sister was married to the murdered man."

Brad was beginning to think that all of the sheepmen and their women were related. He did not know the name of the man who had been beheaded, nor the name of his wife, and he didn't know if he wanted to know. He missed Felicity, and he was becoming a part of this Basque community de-spite his instinct to be detached from their troubles and strife. He had a job to do and the sooner it was over, the better, as far as he was concerned.

"We Basques have no nationality of our own, but we are one big family," Joe said, as if perusing Brad's thoughts.

"I'm beginning to see that," Brad said.

"Will you come to the small funeral in the morning, Brad?" Mike asked. He shifted his feet but remained squat-ted, like a bulky grasshopper.

"I'm not much on funerals," Brad said.

"Why not?" Mike asked.

"Grief is hard to take. Funerals have a way of wringing a man dry. And I don't like to see a woman cry."

"But a funeral is a way to show respect, add some dignity to death," Mike said.

"Funerals may be a comfort to widows and widowers of the deceased," Brad said, "but the dead need no such demon-strations. The dead are gone and will never return in this life.

I say my farewells in private and do not need to hear words spoken over someone who has died and is about to be buried six feet in the ground."

"Ah, then, I must respect your feelings, for you have spoken them like a man who knows his own heart."

"I am sorry for those who have died, especially those who died needlessly and senselessly," Brad said. "But I do not need a funeral to grieve for them."

"I understand," Mike said.

"I, too," said Joe. "I think the church wraps the pagan practice of funerals in religious trappings, as if the priest's words can open the gates of heaven for those who have departed this life."

Mike cocked his head and looked at Joe with an odd expression on his face.

"I think we must leave this subject alone," Mike said. "Or else it will become too complicated for this old mind of mine."

"So be it," Joe said, and the night came on with a solemn whisper as if a curtain had descended over the earth. The cook fire blazed and shot sparks up into the darkness where they danced like fireflies until they disappeared like tiny lives snuffed out by time and its endless cycles of births and deaths.

When Brad turned in and pulled his blanket over him, he thought of the day ahead and wondered if there was any meaning to life beyond any single moment of existence. He remembered his parents and how he had grieved for them. It seemed they had left empty holes in his life, places of vacancy where once they had been and to which they would never return. Death was the big mystery, and when he thought of it, life was an even greater one.

There was only one moment and, if that one passed, there might not be another. Beyond that, there was no guarantee that another moment would come. Perhaps life was a matter of luck. Lucky that it happened and unlucky that it would always end.

That night, Brad dreamed of being chased by wolves through a maze of tall pines while he kept reloading a rifle that would not work and only spit blood from its muzzle. He ran up to a man with a sheep's head who taunted him with a large rope that turned into a snake. He came to a cemetery where there were several faceless men hanging from tree limbs, writhing and cracking like giant whips. He stumbled into an open grave that was filled with green water and bubbled up with red smoke that danced with lightning flashes. His pistols fell apart and his rifles had bent barrels and fell away from him, then wriggled off like tiny rattlesnakes.

He fell from a high cliff where cattle and sheep swarmed around a mound of dirt that resembled a fresh grave. He wandered through surreal nightscapes and blazing pastures of rabid flames, pursued by a shadowy man carrying an ax that dripped blood.

When he awoke just before dawn, Brad was exhausted and Joe snored like some wild beast in the dark of the cabin.

He walked outside and stared up at the stars. He saw the white wool of sheep off in the distance and heard the distant howl of a timber wolf. He wondered if the real world was any less dangerous than the dream world, or any less peculiar.

Women's voices floated to him as the sky began to slowly pale in the east. A horse snorted. Smoke streamed through the valley like ghostly wisps, and he smelled the burning pine from the cabin where the hanged man lay, awaiting burial.

There was an eerie calm, and Brad felt a pang of loneliness as he thought about Felicity rising from sleep in their mountain ranch house. Instead of his own cattle, he heard the bleating of sheep and wondered why he was where he was. He felt like an alien being in an alien world.

He felt as if he were still in a strange dream where some part of the night was eternal and the sun might never rise again.

TWELVE

∽

Otto Schneck rode out to speak to his foreman, Jim Wagner, who was breaking up the herd, separating those cattle fat with calves from the steers and the yearlings. He had two men on cutting horses who were doing most of the work.

Wagner was working a mossy-horned whiteface that had turned belligerent. He gave his horse its head after the cow bellowed and began to run toward a thicket of alder along one of the creeks. Schneck caught up to him just as the cow splashed across the creek and trotted into the timber, bellowing its rage at its pursuer.

"Howdy, Boss," Wagner said as he turned his horse away from the creek. "I may have to shoot that cow so we can roast some beef later on."

"She's got a heap of meat on her."

"And she's meaner than a constipated catamount."

"Maybe you ought to run her down on those sheep," Schneck said. There was a bitter edge to his voice.

"Them sheepherders pulled out yet?" Wagner asked.

Schneck shook his head.

"Far as I know, they don't plan to leave."

"Then, we got us a big problem, Boss." Wagner pulled a toothpick out of his pocket. He stuck it in his mouth and worried it from one side to the other. "Ain't enough grass in this valley to feed what cattle are here for more'n a week or two, and you got more head comin' down from Cheyenne in a day or so."

"I expect we'll have another seven hundred head, maybe eight hundred, by day after tomorrow," Schneck said.

Wagner spat out the toothpick and reached in his back pocket for a plug of tobacco. He cut off a piece with his folding pocketknife and shoved a chunk inside his cheek. He chewed for a minute while he shoved the plug back in his pocket and folded the knife and slipped it away.

"You figure an acre per head, at the very least, Snake, and we're already a thousand acres short on what we have here in this valley."

"I know. That's why we have to run those sheepherders back to Wyoming. They're expecting their main flock today and have already got sheep running on another valley they plan to use all summer."

"Didn't that Garaboxosa get your message?" Wagner asked.

"Garaboxosa. I reckon he did not. I sent LouDon Jackson down there to see if them gypsy bastards are making any move to leave. He should be back right soon."

"Well, if those sheep eat up all the grass, you're going to lose a heap of money, Otto."

"You mean I'm going to get a lot of money stole from me, Jim. Lose ain't the word. Way I figure it, them gypsy sheepherders are stealing the money out of our pockets, the food from our mouths. After their sheep get through with a piece of pasture, there's nothing left but dirt."

"Yeah, sheep will eat grass right down to the roots and then dig up the roots. Any place you got sheep, you got nothin' but dust after they leave."

Schneck pulled a pipe from his shirt pocket, and a pouch from his back pocket. He filled the bowl of the briar with strings of thick-cut tobacco, tamped it down, and stuck his pouch back in his pocket. He dug out a box of wooden matches and struck one of them on the sandpaper side. He drew air through the stem while he held the flaming match to the tobacco. Smoke rose from the bowl and through the pipe stem. Schneck blew smoke out the side of his mouth.

Wagner was a short, stocky man in his late thirties with deep lines etched in his suntanned face. He wore a crumpled felt gray hat with a narrow brim and uncreased crown. A red neckerchief hid the wattles on his neck, but from there to his well-worn leather boots, he was all wire and muscle, as tough as a hickory knot. He was from Abilene, Kansas, but had roamed the West since boyhood as the child of a drummer who sold snake oil curatives in brown bottles for a dollar each.

"Seems to me, Otto, you didn't make your message strong enough. Any man who'd die to protect a herd of sheep ain't fit to live."

"I can't kill them all, Jim."

Wagner fixed a baleful brown eye on Schneck.

"Maybe you've done kilt the wrong ones," Wagner said.

"What do you mean by that?" Schneck asked.

Wagner cocked one leg up on the pommel of his saddle, the saddle horn in the crook of his knee. He spat a stream of honey-brown tobacco juice onto the ground.

"Well, with me it would be my saddle horse I'd hate to see kilt. With some men it's their wives. With others it's probably their kids. Every man has somethin' he don't want to lose, no matter what. If the barn's on fire, I'm goin' to drag out my best horse. If the house is afire, I got to make a choice, grab my baby girl or my old lady."

"You'd save your baby, I think," Schneck said, lost in the picture of the burning house and the screams of the woman and her child.

"Maybe," Wagner said. "Tough choice, but if the kid gets burned, you still got your wife and she can give you more kids. You lose her and you got a kid to raise by yourself."

"I see what you mean," Schneck said.

"You kill all of Garaboxosa's men and he can hire more. And you can't rightly kill off all his sheep less'n you pour poison into their drinkin' water. You do that and you spoil the water for yourself and your cows."

"I see the logic of what you say, Jim. It might be hard to do."

"You kill what a man holds most dear, you kill somethin' inside him, that's all I'm sayin'."

Schneck took in a deep breath. His men left their women at home, their wives and girlfriends, and they didn't bring whores to the grasslands. But the sheepherders brought their families with them. They were a lot like gypsies. And a lot like sheep, too. They took over land as if they owned it and left their buried trash and outhouse offal in holes where flies could breed and rats could thrive. To him, the sheepherders were a filthy bunch, and their flocks ruined the land and left it barren.

"Is that Garaboxosa feller married?" Wagner asked.

"I don't know," Schneck said. "But he's the boss of those sheepherders."

"Too bad. If he ain't got nothin' to lose, you can't hurt him."

Schneck puffed on his briar pipe. He savored the aroma of the tobacco mingled with the scent of evergreens and cattle. He watched the smoke turn to tatters and drift off into nothingness against the backdrop of the snow-crowned peaks chiseled against the blue sky.

"I'll have to give that some thought. He hired a man who's raising hell with my men. Don't know his name, but he shot and killed Rudolph."

"I heard. I heard he was fast with a six-gun and that he bucked up against Hal Sweeney and LouDon Jackson."

"He's got balls," Schneck said.

"Might be he's the man to drop, then. If Gara-whatzisname hired him as a gunslinger. Maybe you get rid of him it would take the wind out of that Basque bastard's sails."

"You got a point, Jim. I have that man on my list anyway."

"Maybe Hal and LouDon can take him down. They're both pretty fair rifle shots."

Wagner spat another stream of tobacco juice and returned his leg to the side of his horse. He slipped his boot into the stirrup as if he was ready to ride off and tend to his duties.

"The man to do it is Sorenson," Schneck said. "But I'm not too sure of him."

"How come?"

"I don't know exactly," Schneck said, "but I get the feeling he doesn't want any part of this range war."

"Is that what it is? A range war?"

"It's shaping up that way, Jim."

"They had some bloody ones up in Wyoming and Montana amongst sheepherders and cattlemen."

"And in Utah and Idaho."

"Who won them wars?" Wagner asked.

"The cattlemen," Schneck said and laughed.

"Maybe history does repeat itself."

"I aim to win this one," Schneck said. "I'm just not real sure about Sorenson. He's not one of us. I don't trust him."

"Well, Otto, seems to me you have a choice."

"Yeah? What?"

"Put it to Sorenson. Straight out. Ask him if he'll go after that gunslick and put his lamp out. If he says no, then get rid of him."

"What if he goes over to the other side?"

Wagner turned his horse and spat tobacco onto a cow pie. "Then, Snake, you got to kill him."

"I reckon so," Schneck said. "Too bad, too, because I really like that big Swede."

"You can't like a man if he ain't worth trustin', Otto."

"True enough, Jim. I think I can no longer trust Sorenson."

"I got to get to it, Boss. We got to drive some of this herd onto another valley or we'll be up to our necks in hungry cattle by the end of the week."

"Thanks, Jim. You've given me some food for thought."

"Don't choke on it, Otto," Wagner said and kicked his roweled spurs into his horse's flanks to put him into a gallop.

Schneck watched him ride off and looked around for the errant cow, but it had disappeared into the trees and was no longer making noise in the brush.

He knew he had decisions to make. Garaboxosa was not responding to his threats and had hired a gunslinger to fight his battles.

He needed a man to spy on the sheepherders, to find out who the gunslick was and whether or not Garaboxosa was married and had ties that could be used against him.

He needed a man who could hire on with the sheepherders and be his spy. It would have to be a clever man, a man who wasn't afraid to be on the sly and tell him what he wanted to know.

Right now, he thought, Garaboxosa was short two men. It might be an opportune time to send a man down there to apply for a job as a sheepherder. Did he have such a man in his employ?

Schneck clamped his teeth down on his pipe. He did have such a man working for him. He might be perfect for the job. The man was a Mexican and a damned good wrangler. Surely the Basque bastard could use such a man.

He rammed spurs into his horse's flanks and trotted across

the valley. He headed for the stables. That's where he would find the man he had in mind to hire on with the sheepherders and tell him what he wanted to know.

The day began to seem a little brighter to Schneck. He had a plan, and he would win this war.

By hook or by crook.

THIRTEEN

∽

Brad looked down on the cow camp from the ridge. He had ridden there in the dark and found a place that offered concealment and a good view of the structure that served as a stable for the horses and mules. Ginger was ground-tied some two hundred yards away and Brad was on foot, with a pair of binoculars slung around his neck.

He watched as riders rode out and relieved the men on night herd, saw the smoke from the chuck wagon as the cook prepared breakfast and coffee. Men wandered out in the pre-dawn light from their log huts and relieved themselves. Voices, low-pitched with garbled parts of words and sentences, drifted up to him. He listened to the moans of cattle and the snorting whickers of horses, the braying of a mule.

Pale morning light inched through the trees around him. It crawled up the trunks of the pines and made the needles shimmer with a brilliant green glow. The valley hovered in shadow like a gray lake, and the cattle were stiff statues in mottled brown and white. Shadows moved among the log huts and there were noises in the stable.

After a time, a lone rider emerged from the deep shadows and headed for the timbered ridge. Brad put the binoculars on him and saw that it was Thor Sorenson. Brad shivered in his buckskins as the rising sun drew the cold from the ground, chilling the air around him. He put the binoculars in their case and waited until Sorenson reached the shelf and disappeared into the timber. Then he walked back to his horse, stuck the binoculars in a saddlebag, and mounted Ginger.

He rode Ginger slowly, almost noiselessly. The tracks of Sorenson's horse were easy to follow. The hooves left streaks in the dew-wet tapestry of the forest, and the left hind foot dragged slightly, turning over fallen pine needles and upsetting desiccated pinecones so that their dried sides flashed up at him like out of place articles in a neatly organized drawer full of knickknacks. He kept Ginger at a pace that would allow Sorenson to stay ahead of him if he didn't stop or dawdle. He wondered where the Swede was going, because the timber thinned out, and he suspected they were going to run out of ridge right soon.

The shelf began to slope, and Brad knew that the ridge would descend into what might be another valley. There were few pine trees, and the scrub pines that remained were stunted by wind and hard weather, snow and rain. The trail he was following might have been a sheep trail at one time. It was very narrow and faded as if it had not been used by animals in some time. So the trail probably did not lead to water but had been used as a kind of portage route by sheep in single file.

As he reached more open ground, he caught a glimpse of Sorenson some three or four hundred yards ahead of him, descending along a ridge spine. Beyond, he saw a long wide valley bristling with young shoots of green grass that seemed to have no end to it. It lay in a huge bowl formed by a ring of young mountains that jutted up in a succession of limestone walls that gave it the look of an immense fortress. He saw a hawk floating above the rimrock as graceful as an aerial dancer in slow motion, its wings rising and falling in currents of air, the tips of its feathers like fingers twisting and turning to stabilize its flight, while its feathered tail twitched from one side to the other in order to correct its course.

Moments later, near the floor of the valley, Brad lost sight of Sorenson. He felt a tug of hesitation in his mind and hauled in on Ginger's reins. The horse stopped, and the hawk folded his wings and sank in a steep dive toward the rimrock.

Sorenson was gone, and Brad didn't know if he had stopped or turned to the right or to the left. He waited and listened. He wet his right index finger and held it up to see from which direction the breeze blew. Straight toward him, out of the valley.

If Sorenson's horse was moving, there would have been sounds. The ground on the spine was hard from the constant breezes and winds. There was no trace of snow on the valley floor. He expected to see a mule deer or two, or perhaps a small herd of elk, but there was only a long emptiness with a greenish hue where the grass must have been over an inch high. The high bluffs offered protection from heavy snows and blistering winds, so the grass at that elevation had more of a head start than other places he had seen.

He waited a while longer, wondering if he would see Sorenson reappear in the valley. But he did not. He weighed the options in his mind. A man might turn left as a natural direction to change course. But he also might turn to the right just to fool anyone who might be tracking him.

How smart was Sorenson? Brad wondered.

Did the man know he was being followed? Some men could sense beyond their natural senses and know if there was a bear or a cougar stalking his track. Sorenson might be such a man. Brad knew that he was himself, especially when he was keyed up in a strange place where he did not know the country or the lay of the land. He was also attuned to danger when he even suspected that someone or something might be following him.

Perhaps Sorenson, the woodsman, was such a man.

Brad turned Ginger to the right and gently nudged him in the flanks with his spurs. The horse turned, and Brad let him pick his way over hard rocky ground, reining him over to avoid brushing against the bushes or trees. The pace was such that in a race with a snail, Ginger would have lost.

Ginger's forelegs stiffened as the ground grew steeper. The horse and its rider descended at a more rapid rate through scrub brush and washouts littered with pebbles and sand.

He halted the horse again to listen. The valley floor was only a few yards away. He should have seen Sorenson if he had continued to drop down to the flat. There was no sign of the man.

Sorenson had turned then.

Right or left?

Brad looked off to the right and then to the left. There wasn't a sign of either a horse or a man. The breeze made a soft sound in the windblown trees and whispers in the brush around him. The air seemed to scream of emptiness and silence as if he were hearing a woman sob softly in a faraway room on a bleak Sunday afternoon.

There was just nothing to see or hear.

Perhaps, he thought, he should return to the trail and track Sorenson once again.

But where could the man have gone?

Up or down? Right or left?

Or straight down into a hidden arroyo.

Certainly not straight up into thin air.

Brad almost laughed at his own wild thoughts. But he was trying to decide how Sorenson could have eluded him so easily.

He studied the valley and turned his head to look back up at the wide slope that descended from the ridge. There were few places to hide, even if Sorenson was a small man and even if he'd been riding a pony instead of a horse.

There were tents in the slope, but these were small fissures where melted snow and heavy rains had plowed furrows into the earth. None of them was deep enough to swallow a big man on a big horse.

He rode on and downward, puzzled as he had seldom been before.

Then he heard a noise and saw a horse, Sorenson's horse, rise up from an elk wallow and shake the dust from its hide and saddle.

Sorenson stood up, covered with dust, and waved at Brad.

"Glad it's you, Storm," Sorenson said.

"How did you do that?" Brad asked, a look of bewilderment on his face.

Sorenson walked toward him, leading his sorrel. He patted dust from his shirt and trousers, but there was a patina of fine silt still on his face.

"I trained Monty here to lie down," Sorenson said. "He can do other tricks as well."

"You sure as hell fooled me."

Brad climbed out of the saddle, and the two men stood face-to-face less than a yard apart.

"Wasn't sure who it was. I thought maybe Snake might have sent a man to follow me, maybe put me down."

"Oh, is, ah, Snake, on the outs with you, Thor?"

"He probably is. I'm not one of his cowpokes, and I think he might want me to do some illegal gun work. I let him know that I was only interested in scouting for him. He wasn't too happy with me."

"But you're still working for him, right?"

"I am, but Snake is up to something. He's got something in his craw. He left real early this morning to talk with his foreman, Wagner. He relies on Wagner for advice, and Wagner's as cold inside as they come. His pa was a snake oil salesman and Jim, that's his given name, ran off and joined up with Quantrill's Raiders. So that boy has been to Kansas and left a lot of spilled blood in at least two states."

"What about Snake? Do you know what he's planning to do?"

"I know he's going to need this valley right here in a few days, and he thinks the sheepers are going to want it, too. He aims to drive them plumb out of the mountains. And, with Snake, that means gunplay and dead sheepherders."

"What about you? Are you going to keep working for Schneck?"

"I wish you wouldn't pussyfoot around about such a serious subject, Brad," Sorenson cracked.

"Well?"

"To give you a straight answer, no. If you look at what's behind my cantle, that's my bedroll. All I got in this particular corner of the world. I maybe got half a month's pay comin', but I don't aim to go back and ask for it."

"How much does Schneck pay you, Thor?"

"Thirty a month and found."

"How would you like to work for me?"

"What is it that you do, Mr. Storm? I know you're not up here hunting elk, and so does Schneck, by the way. He thinks you're a hired gunslinger working for Garaboxosa's sheepherders. I'm wondering if that's true."

"Some of it is," Brad said.

"You're a gunslinger?"

Brad shook his head.

"I'm a cattle rancher, like I said. But that's only part of it. Right now I'm a private detective. I work for the Denver Detective Agency, because I'm indebted to them for my herd of cattle. This is going to be my last job."

Sorenson whistled, long and low.

"I never would have figured you to be no Pinkerton," he said.

Brad laughed. Ginger snorted. Monty shook his head and rattled his mane against his neck.

"Not Pinkerton. Head of the agency is a man named Pendergast."

"You want me to work for you, you say. Doin' what?"

"Keep on working for Schneck. Just tell me what he's up to over the next few days. I'll meet you every day about dusk to hear your report."

"Where?"

"I can ride to the rim above the cow camp."

Sorenson shook his head. "We might be spotted there. How about if I meet you at the first blaze above your camp? Know where it is?"

"I do."

"Nobody from Schneck's bunch will go back there right away."

"That's a good place, then. Are you finished up here?"

"I'll tell Schneck this valley's open for now, but he better hurry."

"I'll see you tonight, then?"

"Tomorrow night. I might know something by then."

"All right."

"This might be real tricky, Brad. How much salary are you offering me?"

"Fifty dollars," Brad said.

"Fifty dollars a month?"

"Fifty dollars a week. I hope this job doesn't last a month. I'll give you fifty bucks tomorrow evening when I see you."

Sorenson let out another whistle.

"One more thing, Thor. I can't ride to Schneck's camp to see you, but you can come into the sheep camp if anything urgent comes up. I'll fix it with Garaboxosa and the others."

"You got yourself a deal, Brad," Sorenson said.

He rubbed his hands and clapped them together to rid his palms of dirt.

Brad extended his hand, and the two men shook over their agreement.

"Be careful, Thor," Brad said.

"You, too. I think Snake is going to send one of his men to kill you. Maybe pretty soon."

"I'll watch my back trail," Brad said.

Both men climbed atop their mounts and parted company. Sorenson rode back up the way he had come, and Brad angled off toward the sheep camp, the dead reckoning location firm in his mind.

Now, he thought, he had a spy in Schneck's camp.

He also knew something else.

He had a price on his head.

FOURTEEN

❦

Jorge Verdugo was surprised that Otto Schneck would even notice him, no less talk to him. Yet, there he was, a hand on Jorge's arm, leading him out of the horse stable and into the nearby timber. Jorge had been finishing up one of the stalls on what had started out as a pole barn with a sloping roof, a back wall of logs and logged-in sides rising to a height of six feet. It was a large building, and another worker was in the process of framing in a tack room at the rear with crude, whipsawed lumber of various sizes.

"The stable's looking good, Jorge," Schneck said when the two men were alone. "You're a good worker."

"Thank you, Mr. Schneck," Jorge said in his faintly accented English.

"Call me Otto, Jorge. How would you like to make some extra money?"

"Sure. You want me to bring you more horses or mules?"

Jorge had left Mexico with a string of stolen horses that he had rebranded with a running iron and driven up to Cheyenne, a long and tortuous trip, with three friends who had to fight Indians, white brigands, and mountain passes. He had sold his horses to Schneck, who had promptly hired him as a wrangler, along with his three friends. Jorge was grateful to Schneck not only for buying the stolen horses but also for giving him and his friends work on the cattle ranch.

"Know anything about sheep?" Schneck asked.

"What?"

"Sheep. Ever wrangle any sheep?"

Verdugo laughed, then quickly recovered.

"Sheep? No, I never wrangled no sheep, Mr. Schneck."

"Just like cows, only smaller."

"They make the funny noises. And they smell."

Schneck laughed.

"Well, no matter, Jorge. I want you to join up with those sheepherders in the lower valley and pretend that you're a sheepherder. Just for a day or two. I'll give you an extra twenty dollars if you'll do that for me."

"I don't know, Mr., ah, Otto. I don't know nothing about sheep, and I don't like sheep. They stink."

"Just for a day or two, Jorge. I want you to tell me how many of the sheepmen are married and how many have children. Do you think you could do that and not let on that you work for me?"

"I don't know. You want me to be the spy? For you?"

"That's a good way to put it, Jorge. Now, do you have an old straw hat?"

"Yes," Jorge said.

"You take one of them mules and ride around that valley and come in from the south, like you come from LaPorte or Fort Collins. You tell them you're looking for work and you'll work cheap. You can work with their horses and mules or learn how to herd sheep. That couldn't be too hard. You keep your eyes open and you count heads. I want to know how many women and kids they got there and where they sleep."

"How do I tell you when I know all this?" Verdugo asked.

"That shouldn't take you more than a day or two. If they don't hire you on, you find some excuse to stay there and eat their grub. You tell them you have a family and they're starving. Cry, if you have to. Gain their sympathy. Then, when you know what I need to know, you sneak back up here and tell me all that you see. *Comprende?*"

"*Sí, comprendo.*"

"Leave as quick as you can. I will expect to see you in two or three days."

"I will take the old mule, Rodrigo," Jorge said. "I will wear the straw hat and look poor."

Schneck grinned.

"You got the idea," he said.

The two walked back to the stable. Schneck climbed back on his horse and rode off to survey the other hands tending to the cattle.

~

That afternoon, Jorge Verdugo was riding in a wide circle on an old mule. He came up to the sheep camp from the south and begged Mike Garaboxosa for a job. Mike looked him over and hired him on the spot.

Later that same day, the herd of sheep came down from the north. There were over one thousand head, and their bleating filled the valley as the herders with their border collies separated them into groups. They were led by Felix Oriola, a tough, bronzed man in his early fifties, who had been born and raised in the Pyrenees. He was a bearded mountain man who spoke little but carried a heavy staff that was a badge of his office. He waved it when giving orders, and he wielded it on the backs of men who did not obey him promptly or who mistreated "his" sheep. He had no sense of humor but possessed a fine singing voice, and he knew all the Spanish and Basque songs from the old country. He also played the guitar, and at night, when he played and sang, his men saw a

softer, more sentimental side to him, as tears rolled down
his cheeks when he sang the sad songs of his people. That
side vanished at daybreak when the sheep were rolling over
the countryside like a wooly tide and he whistled orders to
the dogs and yelled at the men.

Felix was not married, and none who knew him were surprised. He was not a man to show tenderness to any woman
but his mother, and there were many who doubted that she,
if she was still alive, would be an exception.

Verdugo had never seen so many sheep in his life and, as
they streamed into the valley, he kept his distance, standing
close to the old mule, Rodrigo, and wondering what kind of
world he had entered just to earn a few more dollars from
Snake.

Mike put Verdugo to work that afternoon, cutting and carrying firewood to camp. He told the Mexican that there was
to be a big feast that night, since Oriola had brought vegetables and fruits from Cheyenne, a large wagonload of food-
stuffs, along with another chuck wagon. They would have
roast mutton and wine and there would be singing and dancing. He told them that they had just buried one of their herders and this was a way to set aside grief and welcome the new
herd.

"You will meet all who are here, Jorge," Mike said. "And,
if you want to work, we will make a Basque out of you. After
all, some of the same blood runs in our veins."

"I am truly grateful to you, Mr. Garaboxosa. My poor
family is starving, and I need the money."

"And you shall earn every centavo, my Mexican friend.
We thrive on hard work."

Verdugo found himself liking the man he had been hired
to spy on. He saw the women crowd around the wagon that
carried the vegetables, fruits, and wine, eagerly unloading the
goods and carrying them to the various huts in their aprons.
Children laughed and ran about, helping to carry the smaller

items, trailing small puppies in their wakes and laughing all the while.

The sheep camp, Verdugo soon saw, was much different from the sober cow camp. Here, there was life and laughter, and yes, even joy. But he knew that the cattlemen hated the sheepmen, yet he had not taken sides. He would do his job, but he must keep in mind that he worked for the German, Schneck, and should not bear sympathy for Garaboxosa and the sheepherders.

He would pretend to be friends with them, but he would do his job of spying and report all that he found out to Schneck.

Verdugo would do these things, but he would be very sad to betray such people. They were like his own, in many ways, and they made him homesick for Jalisco, where there was much dancing and singing, and much poverty. These people were not Spanish or Mexican, but they looked similar and their ways were more like the ways of his own people, his own family.

He had never tasted mutton, and he did not know if he could eat a sheep.

But he would make friends and try to understand these strange people who found joy in work and spoke a different language.

When he squinted his eyes and listened to their laughter and their lilting language, he saw his own people. He cut the wood and carried it to the log cabins and to the large fire ring near the two chuck wagons. He sweated and strained in the brisk mountain air, and for the first time in a long while, he was happy.

And the sheep did not smell so bad after all.

FIFTEEN

❧

When Brad rode back into the valley, he was unprepared for
the sight of so many sheep streaming out of the timber and
flocking to their new home in the mountains. He sat on his
horse for a long time on the rimrock, staring down at the
flurry of activity around the wagons, especially the wagon
piled high with sacks of potatoes, baskets of oranges, peaches,
apricots, cucumbers, onions, and apples. He listened to the
joyous cries of the children floating up to him like watery,
quivering globes from a bubble pipe, and the women in their
colorful dresses, chattering like magpies in the Basque language, oddly musical and as universal, somehow, as laughter.

Sheep poured into the valley in liquid wooly streams that
flowed over the new grass in a dazzling white cascade, bleating and flexing their boundaries while the little black-and-
white dogs chased deserters back into the flocks where they
were swallowed up on the rippling woolen tide.

He rode down to the valley, taking the path that led him
past the place where he had shot the man in hiding above the

talus slope. He found a path through the woods that led him to the graveyard where there were two crude crosses at the head of two fresh mounds of dirt. The crosses were made of straight limbs nailed together. Someone had cleared away much of the brush and small saplings to make a level space, but had left the tall pines and a graceful pair of spruces. A little farther on, in a less than ideal place, there was another grave, unmarked, and he surmised that this was the place where the sheepmen had buried the would-be bushwhacker.

As he passed that grave, there were signs that at least one human had defecated on the grave. There would probably be more such deposits made by the angry men in the camp. He rode to the stable, which was only a large lean-to with log sidewalls where large twenty-penny nails had been driven so reins and ropes could be looped to hitch up the animals. There were some barrels sawed in half and tarred to hold water and feed.

He dismounted, led Ginger inside, dug out a halter from his saddlebag, and hitched him to a pair of offset nails where one of the barrel halves served as a watering trough. He dug into a sack of grain, corn, and wheat and placed it in another barrel half, which he moved within range of Ginger. The horse began to nibble on the grain while Brad unsaddled him. He hung the reins and his canteen on a lone nail higher up, set his saddle on its side next to the foundation log, and lugged his saddlebags, rifle, and shotgun to the log hut he shared with Joe Arramospe. He sat them next to his bedroll and walked outside to help unload one of the supply wagons.

Brad picked up a stack of blankets and asked a woman standing near him, "Where do you want these?"

The woman laughed and waved a finger at him.

"No, no," she said. "You leave in wagon."

"Huh?"

"No take blankets. Blankets stay. Tents stay."

He set the blankets back down in the wagon and looked at the other items in the bed.

There were small tents, axes, saws, ropes, boxes of matches, sacks of beans, flour, sugar, and baskets of apples, apricots, and other fruits.

Leda walked up to him and pushed him away from the wagon. She, too, wagged a finger at him.

"This wagon for women," she said.

Other women walked over and surrounded him and the wagon. They all had smiles on their faces, indulgent smiles, as if they had just caught one of their children with his hand in the cookie jar.

Brad looked around and saw Mike staring at him. Some of the children wandered over and joined the women, tugging on their mothers' skirts. A small girl in pigtails had a wide grin on her face and looked at him as if he had trespassed on sacred ground.

"I don't understand," Brad said to Leda.

She took his arm and led him away from the wagon, away from the others who were all staring at him as if he were the village idiot.

"Mr. Storm," Leda said, "that wagon for us. We go tomorrow. In morning, we all go to camp on river. Tonight, we eat much. We dance. We sing. Then, we all go to river."

Brad listened to her and saw the others still looking at him with baleful eyes and twisted grins.

Mike walked over and put an arm around Leda. He hugged her, and she kissed him on the cheek.

"Did I do something wrong, Mike?" Brad asked.

Mike stepped a foot away from Leda. He looked at Brad.

"No, but that wagon there is for the women. Two of my men will drive it downriver to a camp where they will stay. All of the women and children are leaving in the morning. We have work to do, and they must go where they are safe."

Brad nodded that he understood.

"I feel stupid," he said.

"Not stupid," Leda said. "You my hero. You hero to all, Mr. Storm."

Brad looked helplessly at Mike.

"I feel like a fool," Brad said.

Mike opened his mouth as if to reply and reassure Brad, but Leda shushed him.

"You go, Mikel," she said. "I talk Mr. Storm. Go, go." She made a brushing motion with both hands. Mike turned and left to join his men.

Leda slid Brad's arm in the crook of her own arm and the two walked over to a stack of logs. She pushed him down onto one of them and sat beside him.

"English no good," she said. "You please forgive."

"Your English is good enough, Mrs. Polentzi."

"You call Leda. No Mrs. Polentzi, eh?"

"All right, Leda. But you must call me Brad, then."

"You listen, eh? Brad." She smiled. "We Basque people. Men tend the sheep. Women cook the food. Mikel, he take the sheep to other valley. Send women and children to camp on river. The men come back when leaves fall and get women and little boys and girls. We wait for the men. You find man who killed Eladio and my Rafael. You kill him. Make Leda very happy."

"I will do my best, Leda," he said.

She patted him on the hand.

"You hero," she said.

Brad wished he were anyplace else but where he was. He was touched by Leda's sincerity, but he was uncomfortable sitting there with Polentzi's widow. He felt out of place. Yet he knew that she probably needed to talk, that she was still grieving for her husband.

As they spoke together, Verdugo approached. He carried a log in his arms. He put it on the back of the pile, out of sight of Leda and Brad. He waited and listened as the two continued to converse with each other.

"Tomorrow," Leda said, "I go with other women and children down to river camp. When you kill Snake, you come and tell me."

"I might just capture Snake," he said. "Take him to jail."

"You bring Snake to river camp. I kill him."

"I couldn't do that," he said. "If I catch him, he must stand before a judge. He must have a fair trial."

"Snake not give Rafael fair trail. Not give Eladio fair trial."

"No, but that's the law. I am a detective, and I am sworn to uphold the law."

"Bah," she said and spat into the dirt. "There no law here. No law for Basque in America."

"That's not true, Leda," he said. "The law says that all men are equal in its eyes."

"Law blind, no?"

"The law isn't blind, Leda. Justice is blind. That is the lady with the scales in her hand. The statues, you know?"

"I know," she said. "Law, justice. No justice for Basque. No law."

Verdugo slipped quietly away. He knew that the women and children were leaving in the morning. They were going to some camp down on the Poudre. He could tell that to Schneck and collect his twenty dollars and forget about these people and their sheep.

Brad saw, out of the corner of his eye, the man who walked into the woods. He knew that he was a Mexican, not a Basque, but that was all. He tucked the information away in a corner of his mind. He thought it strange that Mike would have a Mexican working for him, but perhaps he was hired to free up the Basque herders.

"You come tonight," Leda said. "You eat with Leda. We dance, eh?"

"Yes, I'll dance with you, Leda. I'm very sorry about your husband."

"You kill one man, but Mikel say he not Snake."

"No, he wasn't Snake, but he worked for him."

"Cattlemen no good," she said.

"They do not like sheep eating the grass up here. Not all cattlemen are bad. I am a cattleman."

"I know. Mikel, he tell me. But he say you different. You detective."

"This is my last job as a detective. I am going back to my cattle ranch after I catch Snake."

"You catch him," she said. "You kill him. You kill Snake."

He started to protest, but she got up and walked to where the women were standing. They were all watching the sheep that swarmed into the valley.

Brad spotted Mike and Joe. He got up and walked over to them.

"Where are you putting all these sheep, Mike?" he asked.

"There is another valley beyond this one," he said. "Higher up, maybe a thousand feet higher. They will go there for a month or so, then come back here."

"I think I saw that valley this morning," he said.

Brad pointed in the direction of the valley where he and Sorenson had met up and talked.

"Yes," Mike said. "Big valley."

"I think Snake wants that valley for his cattle," Brad said.

"Well, we will be there. We will not let him come in with his cattle."

"First come, first served," Joe said.

"You might have a fight on your hands."

"How do you know this, Brad?"

"I made a friend who works for Snake," he said. "He is not a cattleman. He's a scout. He doesn't like Snake, and he has agreed to work for me. As a spy."

"Are you sure about this man?" Joe asked.

"I'm sure," Brad said. "And, speaking of that, who is that Mexican chopping wood for you?"

"He came and asked for work. I have lost two men. I put him to work," Mike said.

"Where did he come from?" Brad asked.

"Fort Collins, I think."

"Well, keep your eye on him. He could be a spy for Snake."

The expression on Mike's face changed. Joe frowned.

"Maybe," Joe said. "But why? Snake knows we are here. He knows we have many sheep. Why would he send a man to spy on us?"

"I don't know," Brad said. "And that's what worries me."

He decided that he would find out more about the Mexican that night when everyone was drinking and eating and dancing. He would talk to the man and see if his answers were honest and trustworthy. After all, he told himself, he was a detective and it was his job to gather information, to detect. He might as well earn all of his pay as long as he carried a badge.

That night the revelry started.

There was no sign of the Mexican, and Brad did not even know his name.

But he now knew one thing. The man was a spy, and Snake had sent him.

Tomorrow, Brad said to himself, he would ask Sorenson about him.

For now, he could enjoy himself dancing with Leda and the other ladies before their departure in the morning.

It was a happy evening, though tinged with a deep sadness, too.

In the shadows, beyond the blazing fire, the lanterns, the guitars, and the wagon sheets, there hovered the shades of the two dead men, the one who had been beheaded and the one who had been hanged.

Brad felt the chill, but it was not entirely from the night air and the breeze that blew down from the high peaks.

It was the chill of death and the darkness of the road ahead where danger lurked and men plotted and planned murder most foul.

SIXTEEN

❧

Jorge Verdugo rode in to the Schneck camp late that night, put up the mule, and knocked on the door of Schneck's cabin. He was tired and wanted to get his report over with and get back to his regular work so that he could forget about the Basques. He had watched them dance to the fiddles and guitars and had stolen quietly away, wishing he could have stayed on with those happy people.

"Who is it?" Schneck's gruff voice boomed through the wooden door.

"Verdugo."

"I'll get the latch," Schneck said.

A moment later, Verdugo heard Schneck lift the latch, and the door swung open on leather hinges.

He stepped into the dark room, heard Schneck pad away from him in his stockinged feet. Verdugo heard the tink of the glass chimney, then the scratch of the *fosforo* as the German stuck the match and touched the flame to the wick.

"Back so soon?" Schneck said as he waved Verdugo to a chair and sat down on the edge of a small, rough-hewn table.

"The women and children are going away in the morning," Verdugo said.

"Going away? Where?"

"To some place on the Poudre river."

"All of them?"

"I think so. Yes. They packed their clothes and put them in a wagon with blankets and tents. Many hundreds of sheep came there today. They fill the valley. Many sheep. Maybe one or two thousand. So many they do not have room in that little valley."

"Damn," Schneck said. He walked over to a nail where his pants were hanging. He patted the pockets and then pulled out a gold watch on a chain. He carried it over to the lamp and looked at the time.

"Midnight," he said.

"Will you pay me the twenty dollars, Otto?"

"Yes, yes, but not now. Tomorrow. I want you to wake up Jim Wagner, tell him to get his ass over here quick. Then find Sweeney and Jackson. Tell them to get dressed and ready to ride."

"Yes. I will do that," Verdugo said. He felt an onset of nerves as if he were doing something illegal. He was not a nervous man, but he knew something was wrong for Schneck to send him to wake up the foreman and two other men.

"Then, saddle all our horses. Have them ready, Jorge, in twenty minutes. Can you do that?"

"Four horses, no."

"Get some help. Make sure those saddles are cinched up tight."

"I try," Verdugo said.

"Do it."

There was no sympathy or understanding in Schneck's expression. His neck was bulged out like a bull's, and he was already pulling on his pants and reaching for a shirt.

Verdugo left before Schneck could give him any more orders. He ran to the cabin where he knew Wagner bunked with several other men. He felt sweat drip from his armpits and lave his face.

Wagner was grouchy when Verdugo shook him awake and grumbled until he told him Schneck had ordered him to saddle four horses.

"You'll find Ned and Percy bunking in the second hut to the left of this one. Get them to help you saddle the horses," Wagner said. "Did Snake say what he wanted?"

"No," Verdugo said. "He just wants the horses saddled quick."

"Shit," Wagner said as he pulled on his boots. He stood up and took his gun belt off a nail on the wall as Verdugo left the dark cabin and raced to where Percy Wibble and Ned Kingman slept. Wagner grabbed his rifle from where it stood in a corner and hefted his saddlebags, slung them over his shoulder.

Wibble and Kingman were difficult to wake up. They cursed Verdugo and swung at him from their bedrolls. When he told them that they had to saddle horses for Wagner and Schneck, they got up, rubbed rough granules from their eyes, and swore the entire time they dressed. They stumbled out into the darkness and trotted to the stables. Cattle groaned and grunted and the moon glistened on their spines like quicksilver, splattered their amoebic shadows as they moved and grazed on the short grass.

Verdugo knew where Sweeney and Jackson were and roused them from sleep with a jabbing finger to their chests. They were both hopping mad until he told them that Schneck was on the warpath and he needed them to ride with him.

LouDon Jackson belched and his breath was sour beans and onions that splashed against Verdugo's face and made his stomach twist and roil with bile.

"Why in hell does Schneck want us to ride with him?" Jackson muttered as he donned his jacket.

"Hell, you ought to be damned glad he did, LouDon," Sweeney said. "It means that he still trusts us and we ain't in trouble even if it's after midnight and colder'n a well digger's ass outside."

"Halbert, I don't need you answerin' all my questions," Jackson said.

"Well, you asked."

"I was just askin'. I wasn't talkin' to nobody."

"Maybe Snake don't trust us no more," Sweeney said.

"Why not?"

"Because we . . . oh, hell, I don't know. Maybe it has somethin' to do with that stranger who shot Grunewald."

"Hell, that's old business, Halbert," Jackson said. He plunked on his hat and went outside. He saw that Verdugo was running toward the stables as if his life depended on it.

Sweeney followed a few seconds later, running to catch up. Both men shivered in the sudden chill as freshets of a light wind poured into the valley from the snow-flocked mountain range glistening in the moonlight like some towering fortress with whitewashed ramparts.

Schneck looked at the men assembled in his hut. He wore his six-gun and held his rifle across his lap as he sat on the table.

"What's up, Otto?" Wagner asked.

"I'll tell you what's up, Jim. All of you. Those damned sheepherders have run in a couple thousand sheep and they got to find more graze. Graze that belongs to us, by God, when my main herd gets here day after tomorrow."

"Maybe tomorrow," Wagner said. "It's after midnight."

"I know what time it is, Jim. Just shut up and listen. We don't have a hell of a lot of time."

"Where we goin'?" asked Sweeney, unmindful of Schneck's command, apparently.

"We're going to the Poudre," Schneck said. "We're going to ride down it and hide in the aspens and pines until those

foreigners come down it with their wagons and shit, and then
we're going to blow them all straight to hell."

"Huh?" Jackson husked.

"You heard me. Gun work. Bring plenty of bullets for both
your rifles and your pistols. That damned Garaboxosa didn't
listen to me, so now I'm going to teach him a lesson. A hard
lesson."

"I take it we ain't killin' no sheepherders, Otto," Wagner
said.

"You're pretty canny, Jim," Schneck said. "No, we ain't
killin' sheepherders this damned day. We killed two already
and that Basque bastard didn't get the message."

"Who are we killin' exactly?" Sweeney asked.

Schneck shot him a look that was full of daggers.

"His women and kids, that's who," Schneck said.

Jackson swore under his breath. Sweeney looked as if he
had been kicked squarely in the balls. He tightened up all
over as though someone had pulled a string in his backbone.

"Christ, Otto," Wagner said. "That's a big step. Women
and kids."

"It's the only way I can get Garaboxosa's attention, Jim.
He won't listen to reason. If he runs his sheep on that pasture
land we need, we'll have to hunt all over the Rocky Mountains for enough graze to last the summer. We'll lose time
and we'll lose money, and our cattle won't get fat."

"You have a point, Otto," Jim said. "I just wish . . ."

"If we kill all his men, Garaboxosa can hire more. He
can't get his women and kids back. It's the only way. Now,
let's mount up and make sure you all got plenty of cartridges."

"How many people are we talking about, Boss?" Jackson
asked.

"I didn't get a tally, but a dozen or so, maybe."

"Should be easy pickin's," Sweeney said. "At least them
womenfolk won't be shootin' back."

"Don't be so damned sure, Halbert," Schneck said. "Those

Basque women are tough as hickory. Just pick your targets and don't leave any witnesses alive."

"All right," Sweeney said, that string up his spine loosening a little.

"All right," Schneck said, "let's go. It's a long ride down there and we need to find a good spot before they come down the mountain."

The four men left the cabin and walked to the stables.

Verdugo, Wibble, and Kingman were waiting outside with the four horses all saddled and pawing the ground. Moonlight pewtered their faces and bodies so that they looked ghostly.

"You don't need us to go with you, Boss?" Kingman asked.

"No, not this time. But come dawn, you be on your guard. No telling what those Basques will do when we teach them a lesson."

"Otto," Verdugo said, "I did not tell you before, but I saw that gringo, the one they call 'Sidewinder.'"

"Yeah?" Schneck said.

"He is a detective, and he is the one who killed Rudy."

Schneck wiped a hand across his mouth.

"Sidewinder, huh? Well, we'll see how he stands up to a Snake."

"Yes, sir," Verdugo said.

"Keep an eye out, boys," Schneck said as he dug his rowels into his horse's flanks. The men rode off across the valley, four abreast.

Verdugo watched them go and he shuddered inside.

He knew where they were going and what they were going to do, even though Schneck had not told him.

He felt sorry for those poor women and children who would die. He wished there was something he could do. But he could not stand up to a man like Schneck. Nobody could. He was too strong, too tough, and too lean. He was *muy macho*. Men like Schneck did not back down. When they

wanted something, they got it, and Verdugo knew that Schneck would show no mercy.

He crossed himself. Tomorrow, when he awoke, he would
pray silently for the souls of those women and children he
had seen laughing, playing, and singing as if none of them
had a care in the world.

Tomorrow. Today.

As he mucked out the stable, Verdugo wept. The tears
streamed down his face and he did not wipe them away.

Off in the distance, a wolf howled, and it was the loneliest
sound he had ever heard.

SEVENTEEN

❧

Vivelda Udaberri was a curious young woman. She was also very observant and, some said, too curious for her own good. She was a raven-haired beauty with warm brown eyes that missed very little. All afternoon she had been watching the Mexican, Verdugo. She had first caught sight of him when he was cutting wood for the evening campfire. She noticed him even more when he stood behind the pile of cut logs listening to the American, Brad, and her friend, the widow Leda. She thought that was very curious, but she said nothing at the time.

After that, she shadowed Verdugo everywhere he went. She was very careful so that he did not see her watching him so closely. She saw him at supper and noted that he did not eat much. He spoke but little to those sitting around him, but he seemed most interested in the women and children, and he found excuses to stand or sit near Leda and the detective, Brad Storm. He was very quiet, and few noticed him at all.

Vivelda thought he acted very strange when he slipped

away as the men laid out the wagon sheets to make a small
dance floor and the fiddle player tuned his instrument to
the plucked strings of the guitar. He stepped away from the
firelight and walked slowly to the stables.

Vivelda crept away from the others, all of whom were
watching the musicians and talking with each other. Storm
did not notice that the Mexican had walked away because he
was engaged in a serious talk with a small girl in pigtails
named Oriana and her brother, Zenzo, as their mother, Petra,
stood by with an expression and attitude of motherly pride.
Zenzo showed Storm a shiny harmonica and shook his head
when the American asked him if he could play it. The boy
shook his head and Storm said, "Neither can I."

Vivelda kept to the shadows as Verdugo quietly led the
mule out of the stable, walked it very slowly beyond the range
of the firelight, and climbed onto its bare back.

Curious, she followed him long enough to see him ride toward the downslope of the ridge and disappear. She listened
to the muffled sound of the mule's hooves and determined the
direction the Mexican took. He rode to the top of the ridge
and then turned westward toward the valley where she knew
the cattlemen had their camp.

When she returned to the campfire, the music was in full
swing and dancers swirled and dipped on the wagon sheets.
She kept looking toward the stables to see if the Mexican
would return. She became swept up in the joy and exuberance
of the herders, their women and children, and even danced
with Nestor Tiribio at the insistence of his wife, Renata.

The American detective, whom she thought was very hand-
some, despite his pale skin, danced with Renata, Leda, and to
the delight of all who were there, with Oriana, who beamed as
the tall man glided with her as if she were a princess. She
curtsied afterward to wild applause from the spectators.

The following morning Vivelda walked over to Brad as the
horses were being hitched to the supply wagon and the wagon
that would transport some of the women and the children.

"Did you notice the Mexican man leaving last night?" she asked.

"I know that he left."

"Do you know where he went?"

"I suspect that he rode to the valley where the cattlemen are quartered," he said.

"Did you notice how much attention he paid to the women last night?" Strands of her hair hung in ringlets in front of both ears, framing a face of rare beauty and intelligence.

"No," Brad said. "I figured he was spying for Schneck, the cattle rancher."

"Well, he was. I fear that we might all be in danger."

"Why?" Brad asked.

"I do not trust that man they call 'Snake.' He has already murdered two men in the most horrible way."

"Yes, that's true. But you and the other women and all the children are leaving this morning. You will be safe if Snake mounts an attack on us up here."

"I wish you were going with us. I think I would feel a lot safer."

"You won't be far away, Vivelda," he said, "and two of Mikel's men are escorting you."

"Yes, Fidelio and Benito will take us to our camp, but they won't stay. Benito is just a boy. He has but eighteen years."

"I'm sure they will take good care of you," Brad said.

"I would feel much safer if you came with us. You have the experience. I have heard that you are very fast with a gun, Mr. Storm."

"Being fast doesn't mean as much as you think. It helps, but a good aim is what a man needs when he pulls a gun. The men going with you are good shots or Mikel wouldn't trust them to see that you got to your destination safely."

"Come on, Vivelda," Leda called from the passenger wagon. "We are leaving. Hurry."

"I must go," Vivelda said. "Good-bye, Mr. Storm."

She stood on tiptoe and kissed Brad on the cheek, then

dashed away. Leda and another woman helped pull her up into the wagon.

The wagons pulled ahead with Benito and Fidelio on horseback, riding flank on the passenger wagon. Brad saw that they were packing pistols, rifles, and short shotguns. The women and children all waved to the herders gathered to say farewell.

Mike walked up to Brad.

"We're driving the sheep, most of them, to that other valley, Brad. It'll take us at least two days to get them all over on the new graze."

Brad looked at the ocean of sheep that were slowly moving as they pulled at shoots of grass, ragged by the small shepherd dogs that did not yap or bark, but nipped at the slow ones and kept the sheep from straying.

"Keep your eyes peeled, Mike."

"We will. I'll breathe easier with the women and children gone and safe from Schneck downriver."

"I'll know more about Schneck's plans and whereabouts after I see Sorenson again sometime today."

"I hope you get him, Brad. Schneck, I mean."

"I know who you mean. I can't ride up there blind or I'd be on my way. Sorenson will give me an idea of how to corral Schneck and maybe clap him in irons."

"Clap him in irons?"

"A figure of speech," Brad said. "Handcuff him or hog-tie him and haul him down to Denver to stand trial for murder."

"Good luck," Mike said.

"Thanks," Brad said as Garaboxosa walked away toward the herders who were waiting for orders.

The wagons disappeared down the road that led through the timber and over to the Poudre. Soon, he no longer heard the rumble or the clatter of their wheels. There was only the bleating of the sheep as the flocks kept moving toward the trails that would lead them into the big valley where they would spend the summer and drop their spring lambs.

He had the uneasy feeling that there was trouble just waiting to happen when the sheep reached that other valley. Schneck was not a man to allow sheepherders to graze their flocks on land he had already staked out for his cattle.

He wished he could just ride up there and brace Schneck, call him out, and let the chips fall where they may. But he was outnumbered and unfamiliar with the cattleman's routine.

He would wait for Sorenson to show up and then plan his next move.

One thing was sure. He didn't have much time if he was going to prevent a bloody range war. Once those sheep hit that valley, Schneck would be hopping mad. He would stop at nothing to drive the sheepmen out of the mountains.

"Hurry, Thor," he said to himself.

The sounds of the sheep seemed to him like the ticking of a gigantic clock. And the sheep were as oblivious to the danger as the herders who guided them toward an uncertain destiny.

EIGHTEEN

∽

Sorenson saw Schneck and three other men mount their horses and ride off. He watched as Verdugo turned and walked back into the stables while the other men returned to their bunks, shadows in the moonlight, furtive figures in a strange nightscape. He had been awake when the Mexican rode up on his mule and pounded on Schneck's door.

He couldn't hear what the two men talked about, but he was wide awake when Verdugo awakened all the others and they gathered in Schneck's hut as Verdugo and two other men went to the stables and saddled four horses. He saw Schneck, Wagner, and two other men walk to the stables carrying rifles and packing iron on their hips.

They were going somewhere, he knew, and there would be shooting. But where?

Sorenson bunked alone under a small lean-to he had built himself, with spruce boughs interwoven for a tight roof. He was sheltered in a stand of pines behind the log dwellings.

From there he had a good view of the cabins in daylight and a fair glimpse of them at night. He preferred sleeping alone with only the sounds of the night creatures and the wind, rather than the snoring of other sleepers. From his vantage point, too, he could hear when men arose to relieve themselves or rise up to take the midnight watch. He often could hear the night riders singing to the herd and he found this a soothing sound, as well, since most of the voices were pitched low and came from far away. He felt at home with the yodeling carols of coyotes or the occasional howl of a lone wolf. Sometimes he heard the cough of a cougar as it prowled through the trees sniffing the scents of cattle and men as it moved on soft padded feet among the silent evergreens.

He slept with his clothes on, his rifle and pistol next to his bedroll.

After he saw the four men ride off and disappear in the darkness, Sorenson arose and put on his boots. He strapped on his gun belt outside of his shelter and walked toward the stables. As he drew near he could hear Verdugo inside, the clink of an empty airtight against the wooden grain barrel, the snort and whinny of horses, the soft bray of the mules. He stuck a chaw of tobacco in his mouth and waited outside for Verdugo to leave the stable.

He did not have long to wait.

The Mexican jumped when he saw the silhouetted figure of Sorenson standing there, hatless, a foot taller than he.

"What have you been up to, Jorge?" Sorenson asked.

"Huh?" Verdugo looked rattled and uneasy in the pale wash of moonlight over his face.

"I saw you ride up on that mangy mule an hour ago. Where in hell were you?"

"That is none of your business, Thor," Verdugo said.

"I'm making it my business, Jorge. I want to know where you were all day and what you were doing."

"I was working for Snake, like always."

"Yeah, but doing what?"

Sorenson moved a step closer to Verdugo. His manner was plainly menacing and Verdugo's eyes widened and looked from right to left, as if seeking to escape Sorenson's withering gaze. He was unarmed, and the bullets in the Swede's gun belt gleamed like lethal jewels.

"I do not think Mr. Schneck wants you to know what I was doing for him."

"Well, damn it, I want to know and you'd better tell me or I'll thrash you within an inch of your life."

Verdugo huffed out a breath, an exasperated breath. Sorenson was taller than he and outweighed him. He was also packing iron, and Jorge didn't have so much as a knife on him.

"I went to the valley where the sheep graze. Schneck sent me there."

"Why?" Sorenson asked.

"I—I do not like this talk. I cannot tell you. I will not tell you."

"You'll tell me, Verdugo, or when I finish busting your mouth, you won't be able to talk at all."

"Do not threaten me, Sorenson. You are not with the cattle. You are only a scout."

"Only a scout? Why, you little Mex weasel, I work for Schneck same as you, and I want to know what you were doing down there at the sheep camp."

"Ask Schneck," Verdugo said.

"I'm asking you. I know Schneck and Wagner rode out of here a while ago. So, you tell me what you were doing down there with those sheepmen."

Sorenson grabbed Verdugo's collar and jerked him close to him so that their faces were inches apart. Verdugo tried to pull away, but Sorenson's grip was too tight. He could feel the clenched fist pressing against his throat.

"Spit it out, Verdugo. What were you doing down at that sheep camp?"

Sorenson pushed his fist against Verdugo's Adam's apple and the Mexican gagged and choked.

"I do the spying," he spluttered as he gasped for breath.

"Spying. On who?" Sorenson's anger was building and Verdugo could feel his rage, smell it on his breath. He cowered and raised both arms, clamped his hands on Sorenson's wrists, trying to break free.

Sorenson slapped Verdugo's arm down and shoved him against one of the poles of the stable. They both heard it creak under the strain.

"All right," Verdugo said, "I will tell you. Snake wanted me to watch the women and tell him where they slept at night."

"The women?"

"Yes, the women and their little kids."

"Jesus," Sorenson muttered. "Did you tell him?"

"I—I told him that the women and kids was going away in the morning."

"Going away? Going away where?"

"Let me go," Verdugo pleaded. "Let me go and I will tell you. But Schneck will fire me. Or kill me."

"I'll kill you if you don't tell me what I want to know. Where are the women and children going?"

"I do not know. To some camp place down on the Poudre. They have the wagons and the food and tents. The men do not want their wives and kids to stay there no more."

"Is that where Schneck and Wagner are headed now?"

"I—I think so. Sweeney and Jackson went with them."

"And what does Schneck plan to do, Verdugo?"

"I do not know. He did not say."

"He might not have told you, but you know, don't you? You know where Schneck is going and what he's going to do?"

"No, I do not know." Verdugo started to step away, but Sorenson grabbed the front of his shirt and pulled him back.

"Leave me alone," Verdugo said and struggled to free himself from Sorenson's grip on his shirt.

"Damn you, Jorge. You tell me all of it, or else."

"I do not know anything. Schneck, he don't tell me."

"You were there when he told Wagner and the others, though, weren't you?"

"I did not hear what Schneck said."

"You're a damned liar. I want to know what he said to Jim and the other two men who rode out with him. I know you heard every word Schneck said."

Verdugo shook his head, and Sorenson ran out of patience. He let loose the Mexican's shirt and swatted him across the face with the back of his hand.

Verdugo staggered, then fought back. He lashed out at Sorenson with a clenched fist and grazed his jaw.

"You little Mex bastard," Sorenson growled.

He waded into Verdugo with a left hook to the smaller man's jaw, then followed up with a right to Verdugo's gut.

Verdugo doubled over and cried out in pain. Sorenson straightened him back up with a punishing uppercut and Verdugo's head snapped back with the sharp sound of a crack. His eyes rolled in their sockets and tears boiled up in them.

"Tell me, you little bastard," Sorenson said and drew back his right fist ready to launch it straight into Verdugo's face.

"He—he is going to kill them," Verdugo sobbed. "He is going to kill all the women and all the little kids."

"The sonofabitch," Sorenson said, and dropped his arm and fisted hand.

"I am sorry," Verdugo cried out. "I am sorry."

"You miserable bastard. How much did Schneck pay you?"

"He has not paid me. Twenty dollars."

"You're no better than Judas Iscariot. You sent all those people to their deaths."

"I did not know Snake was going to kill them."

Sorenson appeared as if he was going to walk away, but when he turned back to Verdugo, he went into a crouch and slammed a fist square into Verdugo's jaw. He knocked the man down.

Verdugo was out cold. His eyelids fluttered but did not open. Sorenson stepped over him and went inside the stable.

He rummaged around in the dark for his saddle and bridle, then led Monty outside. He began to saddle his horse as he listened to the shallow breathing coming from Verdugo.

The moon inched across the sky, and the stars wheeled so slowly they could not be tracked.

When he finished saddling Monty, Sorenson led him to his lean-to, grabbed his rifle, and slid it into his scabbard. He had a ridge to climb, a tabletop to traverse, and another cliff to descend. He wondered if he could make it to the valley of the sheep before the women left. He could not hurry in the darkness. There was too much of a chance that Monty would injure a leg, or an ankle.

When he mounted up, he saw the dark hulk of Verdugo attempting to rise. He was holding one side of his head and appeared groggy.

"You better hope Schneck doesn't kill those women and kids, Verdugo," he said. "If they die, you die."

Verdugo said nothing. He staggered around in a half circle and then fell against a post and braced himself so that he would not fall.

Sorenson rode off without looking back. He didn't expect to see Verdugo again. If he did, he just might make good on his threat.

But the man he wanted to kill was not Verdugo but Schneck.

He wanted to kill him before the bastard murdered those women and their children.

He knew it was a tall order, but with the help of Brad Storm, he just might get the chance.

It was a long, slow ride to the sheep camp and there were clouds rolling across the night sky. They would mask the moon and make the going more difficult, he knew.

He rode with his anger and his fear.

He could not measure which was greater as the high thick clouds plunged the world into total darkness and the stars disappeared, too, and Sorenson had never felt more alone, nor more helpless.

NINETEEN

﹏

It was nearly noon when Sorenson appeared atop the rim-rock, leading his lame horse. Brad spotted him as he stood in line at the chuck wagon, an empty bowl in his hand. He could see that Monty was limping, favoring his left hind leg.

Brad stepped out of line and set down his bowl on a stump next to one of the wagon wheels. He waved at Sorenson. The Swede waved back and then beckoned for him to come and meet him as he headed for the talus slope where he could descend into the valley.

Brad took off in a lope to meet Sorenson as the sheepherders looked on in puzzlement.

Huge snowy-white thunderheads billowed up from behind the distant mountains. They floated like giant balloons over the ridges and valleys, heading for the wide prairie. Their shadows crept across the valley and the few sheep that were still grazing and threatened to blot out the sun. The breeze behind them was stiff and steady, building to a high brisk wind that would sail the clouds far and wide like full-sheeted ships in full sail, antic as seabirds before a storm.

Brad felt the chill as he ran, his boot heels gouging small holes in the soft ground, his soles turning green from the crushed grasses underfoot. As he neared the talus slope, Sorenson stepped slow and careful ahead of his crippled horse, holding Monty in check so that he didn't slide on the loose gravel and further injure himself.

Sorenson's eyes widened as he scanned the other side of the valley in vain.

"Where are the women and kids?" he shouted as he neared the bottom of the slope. Monty crashed through heavy brush on three good legs, his ears flattened, his eyes rolling in fear.

Brad stopped short and waited for Sorenson to make it the rest of the way down to the flat plain.

He tipped his hat back on his head, a worried look crawling across his face.

"They're gone, Thor," he called back. "Left this morning, early. Why?"

Sorenson panted for breath as he came to a stop a few yards in front of Storm.

"Hell, we've got to catch up to them, stop them."

"What?"

"Schneck aims to bushwhack them. He's probably waiting for them down on the Poudre."

Brad uttered a blasphemous oath and squared his hat on his head.

"Can you get me a good horse? Monty stepped into a hole during the night and I feel like we've walked a hundred miles."

"I can find you a good horse. How long ago did Schneck leave?"

"Just after midnight, Brad. There's no time to waste."

"Don't say anything about this to those men over by the chuck wagon," Brad said. "They'll panic and run off this mountain like a pack of rabid dogs."

"Schneck's got three men with him and they all got rifles."

Brad swore again. He and Sorenson walked as fast as they

could with the injured gelding hobbling in their wake. Brad headed straight for the stables.

To his dismay, he saw Mike and Joe look up at them from their perches on a log, their bowls of mutton stew in their laps, puzzled looks on their bronzed-leather faces.

"Uh-oh," Brad said.

Sorenson said nothing. He was still short of breath.

"You can put Monty up under that big lean-to we use as a stable," Brad said. "Do you want some liniment or bandages for his ankle?"

"No time," Sorenson said. "I'll doctor him later. Just get me a horse so we can try and catch up to those women and kids."

"We might catch up to them. They're hauling two wagons and going through rough country along the river."

"Let's hope," Sorenson said as they reached the stable. He led Monty inside, dug a halter out of his saddlebag, removed the bridle, and slipped the halter on the horse. Then he unbuckled the cinch on the saddle and stripped it off Monty's back, removing the saddlebags and his bedroll. He dumped them in a heap on the ground.

Brad took the bridle from him and slipped it onto the dun he had brought down from the ridgetop, the horse that had belonged to the man he shot.

"I recognize that horse," Sorenson said. "It belonged to a puncher named Grunewald."

"Well, he won't need it anymore," Brad said. "The horse is yours now."

"I wondered about that boy," Sorenson said. "That the one you shot dead some days back?"

"I reckon," Brad said.

Sorenson began to saddle the dun while Brad took the halter off Ginger and slipped the bridle over his head.

Mike and Joe entered the shadowy interior of the stable. They wiped stray food scraps from their mouths.

"Going somewhere, Brad?" Mike asked.

"This is the man I told you about, Mike. Thor Sorenson.

He's got a line on where Snake might be and we're going to try and track him down."

"Where?" Mike asked. He walked over to Sorenson, who was throwing a blanket on the dun.

Sorenson turned to look at the sheepman.

"Schneck rode out to meet up with a herd he's got coming up from the Cheyenne Trail," Sorenson said. "We might be able to catch up to him if we hurry."

"I am Mikel Garaboxosa, Mr. Sorenson," Mike said as he extended his hand. "Brad vouched for you, so I am grateful for your help."

"Mikel," Sorenson said as he shook Garaboxosa's hand.

"Call me Mike. And this is Joe Arramospe."

Joe nodded and stepped up to shake Sorenson's hand.

"Pleased to meet you, Mr. Sorenson," he said.

"Likewise," Sorenson replied. He slung the saddle over the dun's back and adjusted the blanket until they were both in alignment. He leaned down and grabbed the single cinch, pulled it up under the horse's belly, and ran the bitter end through a metal ring. He drew the belt tight, made a loop in the leather, ran the tongue through it, and pulled it tight. He tested the seating by pushing the saddle horn back and forth. Satisfied, he placed his saddlebags behind the cantle, tied on his bedroll. Finally, he slid his rifle into its scabbard and made sure it was a tight fit.

Mike and Joe walked over to Brad and watched him saddle Ginger.

"Joe, would you mind bringing my rifle and shotgun out from where I bunk?" Brad asked.

"No. I will get them," Joe said.

"Do you have plenty of ammunition?" Mike asked.

"In my saddlebags," Brad said.

"Do you want any of my men to go with you?"

"No," Brad said as he tightened his cinch. "I think Thor and I can handle it."

"I wish you the good luck, Brad," Mike said.

"Thanks, Mike," Brad said.

Joe returned in a few minutes. He handed the Winchester '73 to Brad and held up the shotgun. He watched as Brad holstered the rifle and hung the sawed-off shotgun from his saddle horn.

Brad took his canteen off a wall nail and hung it from his saddle horn on the opposite side from where the shotgun dangled.

"I'm all set, Thor," Brad said as he led Ginger out of the stall.

"Me, too," Sorenson said.

"Be careful, both of you," Mike said. "I may not be here when you get back, Brad. Joe and I are going to check on the sheep to see if they will all make it to the new valley by sundown."

"I'll find you," Brad said. "Wherever you are."

"Will you take Schneck to Denver if you catch him?"

"In a day or so, yes," Brad said.

"Good. I want to see him before you take him down there to be hanged."

"I'll have to protect him once he's in my custody, Mike. That's the law."

"I know. I won't kill him. I just want to spit in his face."

"I think that's legal," Brad said. He pulled himself up into the saddle and looked down at Joe and Mike.

Sorenson rode up beside him.

"The horse is named Fledermaus," he said to Brad. "Good horse."

"German name?"

"Grunewald was German, like Schneck," Sorenson said.

"What does the name mean?" Brad asked.

"It means 'bat,' I think. Fledermaus is a flying mouse. The Germans have long funny words for things."

"You mean like the Swedes?"

Sorenson laughed.

"Yes, we have the long words, too, and some of them are funny to English ears."

"So long, Mike," Brad said. "Joe." He touched a finger to his hat in farewell and turned Ginger toward the same trail the sheep had come up the day before. Sorenson followed him on Fledermaus.

Brad looked back just before they rode out of sight. He was relieved to see Mike and Joe walking back to the chuck wagon. He was worried that they might be concerned about the direction they were going.

"The wagon tracks are easy to see," Sorenson said as they rode in the shadows of the tall pines over the rough road.

"They're about six or seven hours ahead of us, and we can't ride fast over this rough ground. We'll end up with two lame horses if we do."

"Still, we must hurry," Sorenson said. "Schneck will be waiting for those women and children."

"Yes, I know," Brad said. He gave Ginger his head and the horse walked faster but did not break into a lope or a trot. Sorenson kept up with him, and the two men rode side by side.

Brad looked up at the sky. The lumbering thunderheads blotted out the sun, and they were in shadow. The wind had picked up and the pine needles rustled in the gusts that fingered them with chill groping fingers that carried ice in their veins.

There was a chill in his veins, too, as he thought about Vivelda, Leda, and the other women, the small boys and girls that were heading toward a terrible ambush. He thought of Felicity, too, and was glad that she was far away and not with the Basque people in the wagons.

He felt something squeeze his heart and in the cloud shadows, he sensed a brooding dread much like the portent of an oncoming storm in the very heart of a warm spring afternoon.

He shivered inside his jacket and hoped Sorenson hadn't noticed.

Along with the dread, Brad knew, there was fear. He feared that they would not reach the women in the wagons in time.

He feared that Schneck might be there first.

He looked over at Sorenson. The man was staring straight ahead, steely eyed, his jaw hard as granite.

The road ahead was empty and there was a deep silence in the woods.

Now Brad could hear the wind blowing down from the high country, fierce with warning and filled with a penetrating cold that sniffed through the eyelets in his jacket and lashed at his bare neck, ruffled the brim of his hat and tousled Ginger's mane.

And now the thunderheads bore dark underbellies and the shadows on the trail deepened as layers upon layers of thick, heavy clouds floated below the sun, blocking its rays and its warmth, as if dusk were falling like a curtain over the lonesome mountains.

TWENTY

⤲

Halbert Sweeney cursed the thick stand of young aspen, the rocky ground, his blindness to the path ahead of him. Schneck had put him on point, told him to blaze all trees in his path every twenty yards or so. His arm ached from wielding the hatchet, and the joints in his fingers screamed in pain. One of them had turned numb from the cold and his having to force such a tight grip on the small, dull hatchet.

He knew Schneck, Wagner, and Jackson were at least a mile or so behind him, and he hoped they were fighting brush and saplings the way he had for the past three miles. He kept listening for the sound of the Poudre, but he heard only bird calls and odd noises, probably made by deer and elk creeping through the timber.

The ground beneath the horse's hooves became soft, and Sweeney began to see pools of water created by melted snow. He came upon a small creek that wended its way through the aspen and fir trees. He followed a course parallel to the little creek and, as the sun rose ahead of him, he heard the distant whoosh-whisper of the river. Shafts of pale golden light streamed among the pines and aspen, spraying the lush spruce and graceful fir trees that seemed to be standing on tiptoe to embrace the morning light.

Sweeney wanted to shout with joy as the sound of the river grew louder. Now he could hear it crashing over boulders and swooshing in the narrows as it raced between rocks. The aspen groves became thicker and the pines stood tall and lofty, their tops shining green in the light of the rising sun.

He dared not whoop or holler, but he slashed a blaze on a sturdy pine trunk with a savage swipe of the hatchet.

The ground became more treacherous and rocky, with slippery spots where the horse faltered in its forward progress. Saplings slapped at his face as the horse bolted through a patch of young trees and second-growth brush. Small leafy branches scraped and tugged at his trouser legs and the ground became a bog. His horse's hooves sank in the mud and made a loud sucking sound when he lifted each shod hoof. It was rough going, but he could hear the river as it cascaded in full flight with snowmelt from high in the mountains. He could smell the river now and hear the crunch of rotted wood limbs as they smashed against rocks and tumbled into more obstacles as they hurtled down through foam and swirl, over boulders and sandbars, into riffles and eddies, caught in the swirl of a raging river at full tilt.

Then, he saw it, the Poudre, raging like some wild torrent right in front of him. He rode to the edge and looked up and down the fast-moving stream. He saw the tattered road on the other side, its soil ground up by thousands of cloven hooves, rutted by wagon wheels, and scored by the ironclad feet of horses and mules. He drew in a deep breath and drank in the beauty of the river along a steep drop, its waters blue, green, and brown, beneath white-capped waves that leapfrogged over large boulders and smooth stones that jutted from the water like the humps of hippos or giant turtles.

The sun glinted on the rushing waters, and tiny rainbows

danced in the spray around the rocks. He looked up and saw the huge white thunderheads billowing out of the far ranges, blossoming on the blue sky like gigantic bolls of exploding cotton.

Now, he thought, he would have to find a place to ford the river and then they all would have to find a place to ambush the wagons carrying the women and children coming down from the high valley. It seemed a daunting task at that moment because all he could see was a roaring river surging down a narrow defile, a stream that was nearly all dangerous white water. Yet it rounded a bend farther down where it disappeared in a pile of bubbling foam amid curtains of water spray.

Sweeney waited as he gazed at the white-trunked aspen on the other side, the dense forest behind, and the trickle of another small creek finding its way into the river like some blind, groping talon.

He waited for Schneck, Wagner, and Jackson. Four heads were better than one, he reasoned. They could search up and down the Poudre for a crossing and then hunt for a place to bushwhack the wagons.

He listened for the sounds of his companions' horses, but the roar of the river was too loud. He pulled a sack of smoking tobacco from his pocket and slid up a packet of papers. He removed one and made a trough between his fingers. He poured tobacco into the paper and closed it, rolled the paper tight around the loose tobacco. He stuck papers and sack back into his shirt pocket and licked the leading edge of the paper to seal it. He stuck the quirley in between his lips, dug a box of matches from his pants pocket, and lit the twirled end. The cigarette caught fire and he pulled smoke into his throat and lungs, blew out a stream of blue vapor. He tossed the burning match into the river and saw it die in a puff of smoke and disappear in the roiling waters.

He rolled and smoked two more cigarettes before he heard the snorts of horses behind him, the splash of their hooves on the boggy ground. He turned and saw LouDon in the lead, ducking under a willow branch, his horse fighting the ground and surging forward, his chest bulging and shining sable in the sunlight.

"Ho, LouDon," Sweeney called and waved his cigarette at the man.

"Christ, Halbert, you picked a hell of a damned trail."

"I didn't pick it, LouDon. I just come straight to the river."

"You could have found an easier trail." There were small red welts crisscrossing Jackson's face and a trickle of blood streaming onto his forehead from his hairline. His shirt was freckled with twigs and fragments of green leaves and pine needles. He looked as if he had crawled through a tunnel of timber on his hands and knees.

"Well, there it is, LouDon, the Poudre, and if you want, you can ride straight across and find us a hiding place."

"You couldn't get two feet in them waters," Jackson said. "You'd get washed down, smashed to a pulp, and plumb drownded before you could go another foot."

"Hell, I was just joking, LouDon."

"It ain't funny. That there river's in full flood."

"I reckon it is," Sweeney said, and then he saw Wagner riding through the small trees, his horse's feet sucking up mud with every step. Behind him rode Schneck, one arm up over his face to shield it from the whipping branches of the slender saplings. He bore a look of anger on his face, which was puffed up and marked by linear welts. His neck was bulging out of his collar, too, as if he were ready to do battle.

Jim Wagner halted his horse next to Sweeney and Jackson. He slapped at his neck and mashed a wood tick. Sweeney, who had his shirt collar pulled up around his neck, saw Jim's expression and laughed.

"I got my first tick way back there and I been brushin' 'em off my shirt for the past three hours."

"That's the sixth one I've found drinkin' my blood," Wagner said.

Schneck joined the trio and growled a sullen howdy, then asked: "What are you all jawin' about?"

"Damned wood ticks," Jackson said. "I kilt a passel of 'em on the way down here."

"Just be glad we don't have cow ticks yet," Schneck said. "But the wood ticks are bad enough."

"Yeah," Sweeney said, "you can get what they call fever and rheumatiz from these here ticks."

Schneck surveyed the river. He picked a tick off the back of his hand. He had caught it crawling, with its brown and red back. It had not yet found a vein to bite into and suck his blood.

"We have to find a crossing right quick," he said. "Sweeney, how come you didn't find us a fording place?"

"Hell, Boss, I just got here and thought we'd have a better chance if we all looked for a place to cross."

"Let's get to it, then. Those wagons will be coming down that road directly."

"The river takes a bend down a ways," Wagner said. "That might be a good place if it widens enough. Goin' to be tricky, though, even in shallow water."

"Well, our horses can't swim across this swift water," Schneck said. "We'd all get killed. Sweeney, you lead off and head downriver."

"Ain't much bank on this side," Sweeney said.

"Go through the brush, then," Schneck ordered. He slapped at his neck but came up empty.

Sweeney turned his horse and headed downstream, crashing through tangly brush and supple saplings but staying on rocky hard ground.

He reached the bend and rode beyond it. The river did widen there and was more shallow. The water raced over shimmering pebbles, and fish shadows darted in the shallows, dark shapes with a rainbow's red stripe on their sides. Their backs glistened green when their fins broke the surface and the sun glanced off their oily, slippery skins.

He rode a little farther and saw where the banks began to narrow again. He pulled on his reins and halted his horse. He waited for the other three men to catch up.

"What do you think, Mr. Schneck?" he asked. "Reckon we can cross here?"

Schneck, Wagner, and Jackson all looked at the wide shallows, the swift water.

"Jim, can we make it across here?" Schneck said.

"We can try, I reckon. Them rocks look mighty slippery, and I can see moss on some of 'em. An iron shoe could slip off and founder a horse pretty easy, I'm thinkin'."

"We haven't got all day," Schneck said. "Who's going to try it first?"

"Sweeney's first in line," Wagner said.

Schneck fixed his gaze on Sweeney. Sweeney swallowed hard.

"Halbert, you go real slow," Schneck said. "We'll wait until you get across, then follow your same track."

"How deep do you figger it is right here, Jim?" Sweeney asked.

"Maybe a tad higher than your horse's fetlocks, but lower than his knees. You ought to make it if you hold him to a real slow walk and lean him upstream."

"How in hell am I goin' to lean this horse upstream?" Sweeney said.

Jackson and Wagner laughed. Schneck scowled and looked upward to the sky to mark the sun's path toward the billowing clouds that bloomed overhead.

"We're wasting time," Schneck said. "Go on, Halbert. Ride across real slow."

Sweeney clucked to his horse and tapped his flanks with his spurs. The horse did not want to step into the water and balked. Sweeney took off his hat and swatted the horse between the ears.

"Get on, Hambone," he yelled at the horse. "Git, git."

The horse stepped into the water and its front hooves slid

sideways on the smooth rocks. But it pushed onto hard sand and began to pick its way across the ford. It lifted each foot high. The water made fountains against its legs, shooting up and falling down with each step the horse took.

Sweeney made it to the opposite bank in about ten minutes. His horse clambered up onto the bank and stamped its feet, then shook itself from mane to tail.

"Y'all can come on over anytime you're ready," Sweeney said, a wide grin on his face.

Schneck guided his horse along the same path Sweeney had taken but held his horse in check so that it took him longer, and his horse got skittery out in the middle where the water was deeper and stronger. But he made it to the opposite bank and watched as Wagner and Jackson followed at intervals.

"Now, we need to find a suitable place for an ambush," Schneck said. "Don't any of you ride down the road any more than you have to. And when we cross, LouDon, you be sure to get you a spruce limb and wipe out our tracks."

"Yes, sir," Jackson said.

The four men crossed the road in single file and stayed to the rock-strewn stretch where flooding had left rocks of every size when the river jumped its banks in previous spring floods. Jackson cut a willow branch and wiped out their tracks on the road.

"I wonder where the hell we are," Schneck said after a while.

"There ain't no fresh wagon tracks on that road," Jackson said. "So, we're somewhere twixt our valley and LaPorte."

"You dumb bastard," Schneck said. "I know where we are, but not exactly."

"I lost all track of time and distance comin' through that heavy timber," Wagner said. "But we're still high up, I reckon. And they ain't passed us yet."

"That's what I wanted to know," Schneck said

They rode on, looking for possible places for an ambush

as the clouds swirled in the sky and began to float toward the arc of the sun. A breeze sprang up and lifted delicate spray off the river's whitecaps, and somewhere a mountain quail called a piping strain of melodic notes and then was silent as the breeze stiffened and made the aspen leaves jiggle and twist so that the colors changed, shifted subtly with every cooling gust.

Schneck kept looking over his shoulder at the road, and he fingered the butt of his Colt in its holster. He did not hear anything, but his nostrils seemed to fill up with the cloying scent of blood.

Human blood.

TWENTY-ONE

∽

Brad and Thor stopped to water their horses at a small wood-land lake a short distance from the road. They had not yet reached the Poudre, but they were some distance from the valley they had left. Below the lake was a beaver dam. Water spilled over the dam and as they rode on, they passed several smaller dams and heard the warning slap of the beavers' flat tails as the furry animals dove under their mud-and-stick shelters. Small birds flitted along the tiny stream, and yellow butterflies bounced on the air like autumn leaves. Nymphs skittered just above the water, and some perched on small stones and flexed their dusty, moth-like wings as if they were fanning themselves in the fresh air.

The wide canyon was shadowy with heavy, ash-bottomed clouds hovering just above it, all packed together and floating eastward, propelled by strong winds from miles away.

Brad thought that these were prairie-seeking clouds and would not bring rain to the mountains. He had seen the Rock-ies produce their own weather many times, forming huge clouds and launching them over the highest peaks like sailing ships, only to see them drift off, turn black, and bring darkness and lightning and heavy rains to the plains and the towns down on the flat.

Today seemed no different. The cloud tops were still fluffy and white and the temperature still mild. These were not yet rain clouds. They were just the mountains' way to shed moisture for a parched land beyond their majestic dominion.

As their horses slaked their thirst in the lake, a cow elk, drinking on the far side of the lake, lifted her head and bellowed softly at them, giving off a throaty grunt that startled the two horses. The elk finished drinking and turned and strode off into the timber, the tawny fluff of her tail like some sad and snooty good-bye wave.

Trout broke the surface of the slightly ruffled waters and snatched nymphs and dragonflies out of the air in graceful porpoising arcs and left concentric ripples that spread in ever-expanding circles until they lapped at the mosses and grasses that bordered the shoreline.

"I wonder if this lake has any bass in it," Thor remarked.

"No. Just trout," Brad said. "There are dozens, maybe hundreds, of these little lakes all through the Rockies. I've fished some of them. Never saw anything in them except rainbow trout. But on the streams, I've caught speckled trout and cutthroat trout."

"Taste good?"

"Very good," Brad replied. "I know dozens of ways to cook them, and so does my wife, Felicity. They taste best when you've just taken them out of the water, cleaned them, and put them on a grate atop an open fire, maybe with a sprig or two of sagebrush laid on top of the burning wood. They have very delicate flesh and small bones that come out when you filet them."

"Never tasted such fish," Thor said. "Bass and sunfish is mostly what we have up north."

"Maybe I'll take you fishing with me when this job is finished," Brad said.

"I'd like that," Thor said, and they pulled on their reins and guided their horses back to the road down the steep canyon to the river.

Two young mule deer crept out of the brush-choked creek and bounded off into the surrounding timber. They made little noise as they gamboled away, leaving a cloud of birds flushing from cover.

The two men were silent for a time as they wended their way down the canyon and onto the road slashed into being long ago by lumberjacks and later improved by sheepherders and hunters.

"Why do we talk about fishing and such when we know what lies ahead on this cloudy day?" Thor asked after a time of reflection.

"Fear," Brad said.

"Fear?" Thor acted surprised and glanced at Brad's face.

"We talk about ordinary things because we dread what we might find down this road," Brad said. "The fear is that we might be too late to save those Basque women and their children."

"Are we also afraid of facing Schneck and three of his men?"

"Maybe," Brad said. "The unknown is always a fearsome thing. We can't put a name to it, so we are afraid of it."

"I never thought about it that way," Thor said.

"I keep going over this road in my mind. I wonder where the wagons are right this minute. I wonder where Schneck and his men are waiting in ambush. And all this makes my stomach tighten up and sweat break out on my forehead. Behind all that wondering, there is the stalking beast of my imagination. I fear what I can't see, what I can't know."

"I think I know what you mean, Brad. My imagination has been going wild ever since I talked to the Mex, Verdugo. I keep thinking of the hatred Schneck has for those sheepherders."

"Did you know that when you went to work for him?"

"No, he never mentioned it until he knew the sheepherders were up in that valley. He considered it a personal insult and a threat. He said sheep would ruin the grass forever. He really has a big wad of hate stuck in his craw."

"Hatred can blind a man to both reason and the truth," Brad said.

They prodded their horses into a faster gait, each man living with his own private thoughts, both listening for any sound of wagons rumbling down the road ahead of them. They both gazed at the ruts and saw where the wagons had stopped so that the women and children could go into the woods and relieve themselves. They saw the imprints of small shoes and boots coming and going. Neither man commented, but Brad noticed that the edges of the shoe tracks and the horse tracks were beginning to crumble. At one time, he knew, the tracks were crisp and well-defined. Hours ago. Now, the breeze was turning the top rims of the tracks into dust. The road was drying out.

The road and the river wound down through small, ancient moraines where rocks and boulders had rolled under the powerful rush of flooding waters eons ago. Some of the places were desolate and pools of water still remained near the bank of the river, left there by the first rush of melted snow hurtling down from the muscular slopes of the high mountains.

The river ran fast, whooshing over rocks and splashing through narrow crevices in the streambed, carrying clouds of silt and dirt along with disjointed tree branches, small limbs with tattered leaves still clinging to them, as if it were scouring the earth with its powerful energy. The river widened and narrowed in rapid succession as they rode along its length. Chunks of bank tore loose, and the clods of dirt and grass fell into the maelstrom and were decimated and obliterated within a few yards amid the turbulence. Rocks loosened from the bank and clattered as they fell into the cascading waters before they vanished in silence amid the shadowy shapes of trout grabbing at the grubs and earthworms dislodged from their earthen hiding places.

Brad felt a tug at his heart as he watched the trout flash beneath the greenish waters, snatching easy morsels from the clumps of dirt and grass. They sometimes exploded from the water and gulped down the flying nymphs flapping close to the surface. He thought of how complex life was, with its delicate balance between life and death, each creature depending on others for food and survival.

Sheep versus cattle, he thought. Man depended on both species for food and clothing. Brad was wearing the skins of deer he had killed, and the world depended not only on wool but also on beef and cowhides. Both had a place in the universe, yet neither shepherd nor cowman could meet on common ground and work out a solution to the grazing problem. It seemed senseless to Brad, but he knew that it was the way of the world. If enemies could not be found, enemies would be created, and it was always survival of the fittest. All creatures have to obtain sustenance, and in that delicate balancing act of nature, some must die so that others can live.

There were no winners in the long run, Brad thought. A man might hunt elk and live off the meat for a month, and in the next, he might encounter a bull in the rut and wind up gored and dead. The elk would not eat the man, but it was pushing down on the scales and death was the great leveler in the complex scheme of life.

On the road ahead, they saw a rag doll that must have fallen from one of the wagons. The sight of it wrenched at the two men because, at first glance, it looked like a small child dressed in blue overalls with red hair. Brad's stomach turned until he got close enough to see that it was only a doll.

The two men looked at each other and rode on, kicking their horses into a trot.

Ten minutes later, they heard the crack of a rifle. Then, more shots sounded far down the road and the screams of

women and children floated up to them as if from some unknown cave or dungeon.

Brad put Ginger into a gallop, a grim cast to his face.
Sorenson spurred his horse, too, and the two men raced down
the road filled with a dread larger than the dark clouds floating over their heads.

The rifle shots grew louder and the screams more piercing.

Both men drew their pistols against an enemy they could
not see. But the act gave them some comfort. They were armed
and ready to shoot.

The wind was cold against their faces, and the rims of
their ears reddened with the chill.

They rounded a bend and saw the two wagons askew on
the road, each cocked at a crazy angle with dead horses collapsed in their traces and the outriders sprawled on the road
like fallen scarecrows, the crimson pools of their blood turning as black as ebony.

Small children stood in one wagon, clutching each other,
screaming and whimpering.

And, still, there were the screams of terrified women and
the whipcrack snap of rifle shots in quick succession. Puffs
of white smoke burst from behind trees and blew to ghostly
tatters in the brusque wash of wind that coursed the canyon
and whipped the waves of the river into a frothy frenzy.

Brad's heart seemed to stop, and he felt an iron hand
squeeze it.

The tears came when he saw a small boy blown out of the
wagon, his head in a cloud of blood as if he'd been smitten
by an iron-studded mace wielded by some medieval warrior.

Time stopped at that moment, and everything Brad saw
seemed to be some grotesque tapestry pinned to a stone wall
where there was only blood and the screams of women fleeing for their very lives.

TWENTY-TWO

∽

When Schneck saw the wide moraine next to the road, the bordering timber, he knew that it was the perfect place for an ambush. He found Jackson a place to set up in a choked stand of aspen that seemed a perfect hiding spot. He ordered them all to stake out their horses deep in the woods while Jackson sat there in the concealing aspens to watch the road. They took his horse and led it to a place a quarter mile from the road and hobbled the horses in a small wooded glade behind a huge outcropping of gray rocks mottled with moss and mold.

Sweeney, Wagner, and Schneck hiked back to the road.

"Halbert," Schneck said, "you set yourself up next to the river in that cluster of alder bushes. Sit real still and keep your eyes and ears open. Jackson's off to your left, and you'll see the wagons before he does. Wait until the wagons are real close and then you shoot the horses. Shoot them dead, every one, so that those wagons can't move. Got that?"

"Sure do, Boss," Sweeney said. He walked to the bank

and lay prone in a shallow depression. He laid his rifle out and cocked a shell into the Winchester's chamber. He sighted down the barrel to a point midway between the bend in the road and its imaginary center.

Satisfied, Schneck and Wagner walked back to the line of large aspens on the other side of the road.

"We can shoot from here," Schneck said.

"Standin' up?"

"Yes, Jim. That way, we can move around, pick our targets. Some of them might try to run away."

"You mean the women?" Wagner said.

"Women, kids, the wagon drivers. We need to be flexible so that none of them gets away from us."

"No witnesses, right?"

"No witnesses," Schneck repeated.

The two men stood behind two thick-trunked aspens. They weren't concealed entirely, but they did not present silhouettes to anyone coming down the road. With the big clouds floating overhead, they were in shadow. Both levered fresh cartridges into their rifles.

Schneck also loosened his pistol in its holster, sliding it up and down to make sure he could jerk it free when he needed it.

Wagner was a few yards in front of him. From Schneck's position he could see all three men, which was the way he wanted it. He was the general, the commander in the field, and he saw himself that way. He licked his lips in anticipation of the slaughter to come, and he thought upon the effect the killings would have on Garaboxosa and the other sheepherders.

Maybe that sheepherding bastard will get the idea that I mean business, he thought. I gave him fair warning and he didn't listen. Now, maybe he'll pack up and drive his damned sheep back to Wyoming. I'd like to kill every one of his damned sheep. They have no business eating my good grass. Let all those Basque bastards go back to Spain or wherever they come from. This is America, by God, and here in the West, we raise cattle, not sheep. We don't need their damned wool, either. We grow our own cotton in the South and we got other ways to stay warm.

Schneck worked himself up into a silent frenzy with his thoughts. He held the barrel of his rifle against the tree and flexed his trigger finger just outside the guard. He sighted down the barrel, lining up the blade front sight directly in the center of the rear buckhorn, and squeezed thin air to simulate firing that first shot. He wanted to kill a woman right off. He wanted to see her body turn to stone with the shock of the bullet. He wanted to hear her scream as blood filled her lungs and throat and gushed out of her mouth.

His thoughts began to arouse him sexually. Blood and pain did that to him. He once had a fat mistress that he beat up frequently just so he could be aroused and heighten his satisfaction when he bedded her, plumbing her bruised and swollen depths while she sobbed and moaned beneath him.

He had known many women, and none of them had lasted long when he lived with them. They all left with broken arms, cracked jaws, black eyes, and bruised bodies. Those bruises were the brands he put on them, and he had once notched the ear of a German fräulein just so she would always remember him. He had used the same tool on her that he used to notch the ears of his newborn calves before they were branded.

He thought of those times and the weeping, screaming women as he waited for the wagons to round the bend and come within range of four rifles.

An hour went by, then another. Then he heard the far-off rumble, thump, and clunk of wagon wheels. He felt his heart pump faster, felt his temples throb. His mouth went dry, and he wiped a sweaty palm on his trousers, then grabbed the stock and nestled it against his cheek and sighted down the barrel.

The sounds became louder, and he heard the laughter and

banter of the children, the low voices of the women trying
to control their exuberance while hanging on to the sides of
a rocking wagon.

Then the supply wagon hove into view, slogging along at
a slow pace ahead of the passenger wagon. They seemed to
be in no great hurry. Some of the children were pointing at
the river and counting the small rainbows they saw dancing in the fine mist. All of them were gawking at the river,
marveling at its force, its powerful surges over the rocks and
boulders, the green rush of its waters as they flattened out
before they crashed against rows of rocks jutting from the
shallows.

Two riders flanked the passenger wagon. Two swarthy,
squat men who wore pistols on their old and worn gun belts.
But their rifles and shotguns were lodged firmly in their scab-
bards. The wagoners had no weapons showing.

Closer and closer they came, the wagons and the gabbling
women, the babbling, gleeful children.

Schneck slipped his index finger inside the trigger guard
and slowed his breathing so that it was steady and controlled.

The wagons rumbled close to where Jackson was waiting.

Schneck held his breath. He could not see LouDon, but he
knew he was there in that small circle of aspens. He looked
for the snout of his rifle but could not see it.

Then he heard the crack of the rifle. He saw a plume of
white smoke spew from the trees, saw the sparks fly like
golden fireflies, and heard the thud of the bullet as it smacked
into the chest of the bay mare on the left of the passenger
wagon. The horse tried to rock backward on its hind legs
as blood spurted from a hole in its chest muscle. The horse
floundered and fell to its side with a crash and a tangle of
harness. The horse at its side neighed in terror and wheeled
to its left. Jackson's rifle spoke again, and the other horse
went down with a bleeding hole in its neck. It floundered on
the ground in its death throes like some huge water mam-

mal, a whale flung from the sea. The children and the women screamed in terror as the two horses went down.

The driver on the supply wagon veered to his right, not sure where the shots had come from or what had happened. He looked over his shoulder, but by then, it was too late.

Jackson dropped the horse nearest to him with a shot to its heart. The bullet smashed through the horse's ribs. The horse screamed in pain, a high-pitched whinny that was laden with fear and terror. The animal collapsed at the edge of the road, and the wagon twisted behind it as the driver jerked hard on the reins. Jackson shot the other horse, and Sweeney opened fire on one of the two outriders. He dropped the man with the first shot, then swung on the other one, who was pulling on the stock of his rifle.

Wagner shot both drivers with two quick and perfectly aimed shots. They tumbled off the side and fell to the ground, their hearts smashed to a pulp, their ribs splintered over punctured lungs.

A woman stood up in the second wagon at the rear and Schneck brought his sights in line and squeezed the trigger. He heard the bullet hit, and it gave him a thrill. She dropped like a stone without a sound, and Schneck felt the splash of milky seed in his shorts as he ejaculated. His loins quivered with the ecstasy of the moment, and he levered another cartridge into the firing chamber of his rifle.

The women screamed louder than when Jackson had shot and killed the last horse. The children, bewildered, all began to cry out for their mothers and fathers.

Schneck shot another woman who had jumped down from the passenger wagon and was running headlong down the road straight toward him.

He deliberately aimed for her stomach and heard the smack of the bullet as it rammed into the soft flesh beneath her dress. She threw up both arms and staggered a few feet before she fell and doubled up in pain, unable to scream or cry out. Blood spurted from the hole in her midsection and welled up in a dark pool under her twitching form.

Jackson shot the two riderless horses just for good measure and then swung his rifle toward the women in the wagon.

Sweeney stood up and walked toward the wagons, working his lever as he held his rifle waist-high. His eyes gleamed with bloodlust as he began firing at women who had jumped from the passenger wagon and were reaching up for their children. He shot one woman who had dragged her little girl from the wagon and was trying to duck under it.

Schneck saw two small girls running back up the road as if they could find safety there. He drew a bead on the taller of the two and saw her hit the ground in a flounce of colored cloth. The other girl stopped and squatted down. Schneck shot her a second or two later, watched her little body fall and one of her legs quiver and jerk before all motion ceased forever.

Out of the corner of his eye, Schneck saw a young woman with long dark hair climb over the back of the wagon and run like a deer into the woods.

"Did you see that one, Jim?" Schneck called out.

"Yeah, I saw her."

"We'll have to hunt her down."

"Maybe I'll put the boots to her when I catch her," Jim said.

"Maybe we both will," Schneck said with a smile.

Wagner and Schneck picked out more targets and continued to shoot until they had to reload.

Jackson walked out of his hiding place and held up his hand as he faced both men.

"What is it?" Jim shouted.

"I think I hear something up the road. Horses, maybe."

Schneck and Wagner stopped firing. So did Sweeney.

In the silence they all heard it. There was the sound of hoofbeats from up the road.

Horses coming fast, Schneck thought.

"Get to the horses," Schneck called out and started running into the trees, his rifle trailing at his side like an extra appendage.

Sweeney ran across the road and joined Jackson. The two raced to where their horses were tethered.

Schneck and Wagner were already there. Schneck shoved his rifle in its boot and, grabbing the horn, pulled himself up into his saddle a few seconds before Wagner did the same.

"Where to, Otto?" Wagner asked.

"Just scatter into the woods until we find out who's coming down that road."

"Where do we meet up?" Sweeney asked as he settled in his saddle.

"Upstream, where we crossed," Schneck said. "LouDon, you better hang around and count heads, then let us know."

"You leavin' me by myself?" Jackson complained.

"I need to know what we're facing. You take that pistol and fire two quick shots if you get in trouble. Just hide out and wait, but be ready to light a shuck if you're outnumbered or they come hunting you."

Jackson swore under his breath as the three men rode off into the timber and disappeared. He listened for a time until he could no longer hear them.

He rode closer to the slaughtering place to get a better glimpse of the road but held his horse behind a bristling blue spruce.

He did not have long to wait.

Two men on horseback galloped up to the passenger wagon. They both had pistols in their hands.

He recognized one of the men.

It was Thor Sorenson.

He knew who the other man was. That was the man they called the Sidewinder.

Jackson's throat went dry. He wanted no part of either man.

He snaked his pistol out of its holster and wondered if he dared fire off two quick shots.

And if he did, he wondered if Schneck and the others would even come to his aid.

He held the pistol in his hand, drooping at his side.

He did not thumb the hammer back. Instead, he looked around for a place to run and hide without making any noise. A knot of fear rose up in him and clogged his throat as if it had been stuffed with a dirty sock.

Then, Jackson vomited.

TWENTY-THREE

∽

Brad drew up behind the trailing wagon and scanned the carnage that lay all around him—the dead horses, the bloody corpses of the women and children. Their clothes flapped in the wind. Their faces were wan and tear-streaked, their eyes blank as smoky marbles, staring sightlessly into nothingness.

His stomach tightened into a hard knot and bile rose up in his throat.

Thor rode up beside him, looked around at the slain women and children, then began to scan the woods.

"They might still be somewhere close by," Sorenson said. "Schneck could be watchin' us right now."

"Let the bastard watch," Brad said. "Let's see if anyone here is still alive."

Brad could hear his heart beat. It throbbed in his chest like some night thunder and pounded in his ears like a slow triphammer pounding a bell, thick and dull as cotton. His stomach swirled with the sickness of sudden and terrible grief, as if his own wife lay among the dead and dying. He struggled to find words in his mind that could explain the deep sense of loss when he looked at the small children, children who would never laugh, or skip rope, or run though summer meadows, or swim in blue mountain lakes ever again. His eyes blurred with tears as he dismounted and looped his reins around the silent and stolid wagon wheel.

"You keep an eye out, Thor," Brad said, his voice choked with intolerable emotion. "I'm just going to . . ."

Just then, they both heard a sound from the woods. The sound of someone retching.

"What was that?" Sorenson asked in a loud breathy whisper.

"It sounded like somebody throwing up his chow," Brad said.

"I'd better go check," Sorenson said. He holstered his pistol and jerked his rifle from its scabbard. He jacked a shell into the chamber and rode off into the timber, proceeding at a cautious pace.

Brad walked around, looked at the dead men and at the pitiful sight of the women and children. He heard a low moan from beneath the supply wagon and stooped down to take a look. His heart sank like a lead weight when he saw the woman.

It was Leda, and she lifted one arm when she saw Brad. She looked like a drowning woman stretching her hand out to a would-be rescuer.

"Brad," she breathed, and blood bubbled from her mouth.

"Leda," he said and crawled beneath the wagon. The front of her dress was drenched with blood, though he could not see a wound. He grasped her hand and squeezed it to try and give her some kind of comfort.

"Where are you hit?" he asked, whispering the words close to her ear.

"I—I do not know," she gasped. "It hurts to breathe, and my left arm has no feeling. My fingers do not move."

"Just lie still," he said. "I'll see if I can find where the bullet hit you. It may hurt some."

"Ooooh," she moaned as he touched her shoulder then traced a finger over the mass of blood. He stopped when his fingertip dipped into a hollow depression. He gently pulled apart that section of her dress and saw a blue-black hole in her olive skin.

"You got hit there," he said as her eyes closed, and she looked as if she would fall into a swoon.

She moaned and opened her tear-filled eyes. He looked at them and could see the pain and grief of a thousand years in each of them. She looked old and tired, but there was a fierceness in her expression, too, an age-old wisdom of those who have suffered much in their lives and carried the sadness of a cast-down race in their bloodstream. He saw all that in her eyes and face and was overwhelmed with sadness that mingled with an anger toward whoever had shot her down like a stray dog. Leda was still a young woman, but she had aged in the past few minutes, and he thought how cruel it was to rob a woman of her beauty and dignity with a single gunshot, as if she didn't matter and would not be missed by a single soul in her life.

"Brad," she moaned, "tell Mikel I tried to save the children."

His throat filled with unbidden sobs, and he squeezed her hand.

"You can tell him yourself, Leda. I can maybe patch up that hole, hitch our horses to a wagon, and get you back up to the valley."

To his surprise, she squeezed back, but her hand was weak and he barely felt the pressure of her fingers.

"No," she said, and her voice had turned husky. "I am not long for this world. I know. My fire is dying. I can feel it get small, and there is no longer any fire to keep me warm."

"Don't say that," he whispered. "You can't die right now. You are too young. And you are too beautiful."

"I go to meet my husband," she said. "I know he is waiting for me. I—I can hear him call my name. I hear him calling, Brad. You say good-bye to Mikel for me. You are my hero."

It was a long speech for a dying woman, he knew. She was dying, though, and there was nothing he could do about it. Her life was ebbing away, and soon she would be still and cold like all the others who lay strewn about the rocky road like outsized dolls tossed from a child's toy box.

"I wish you would stay, Leda. You are a wonderful woman. Please stay with us."

"No," she said, and the husk in her voice had turned to a raspy whisper. "We each have our time in life. My time has gone. There is one thing you can do for me, Brad."

"Anything," he said.

"Vivelda," she said, her voice barely audible. "I—I pushed her from the wagon. She ran into the trees. Find her, please. Tell her . . ."

That was all Leda said, all she could say. He thought he could see her breath leave her body just as those ancient Greeks said it did, in a thin vapor that was her soul, her psyche. Her eyes closed and her breath left her, never to return. Her hand went limp in his, and her chest stopped rising and falling. The blood ceased to flow from her wound as her heart stopped.

He felt the tears sting his eyes as he let her hand fall from his.

"Good-bye, Leda," he said in a voice choked with emotion.

He wondered if he should say a prayer for her. No, she did not need any prayer from him. Leda knew where she was going; she was probably already there.

He crawled out from under the wagon and took off his hat in reverence for Leda. He slapped it against his leg as if he did not want to be caught crying or showing sympathy for a woman he hardly knew.

But there was no one there to see him.

He put his hat back on and walked toward Ginger.

That's when he heard a shout from the timber and a rash of angry words flying between two men. One of the voices was Sorenson's.

Then he heard two quick shots.

His blood quickened as he pulled himself up into the saddle.

He heard a crash and wondered who had fallen. Or what had fallen.

A horse neighed, and the stillness of day engulfed him as if the dark clouds had descended and smothered the world around him in a thick, fluffy shroud.

Brad drew his pistol once again and thumbed the hammer back to full cock.

"Thor," he called.

But there was no answer.

TWENTY-FOUR

❧

LouDon's stomach contents splashed onto his boots, his stir-rup, and part of his trouser leg. There wasn't much food left from supper the night before, but there was the stale stench of coffee and the stinging scent of digestive juices.

He knew he had made a mistake, throwing up like that so near to the road.

His horse sidled away from the mess that had splashed on the ground. The animal took just one step sideways as if to avoid the poisonous substance so near its hooves.

LouDon straightened up and wiped his soiled mouth on his sleeve. His stomach still boiled, and he tried to put the stark images of the bullet-ruptured children out of his mind. He could still hear their frantic screams, could still feel the terror in their voices as the rifles cracked and dropped them one by one. He could see the fear on their faces as they ran in all directions as if fleeing from a fire.

Nor could he forget the dark-skinned women and blot out their shrill screams as the rifles barked and bullets punched holes in their breasts, their heads, and their hearts. Such a waste of womanhood, he thought, such a horror.

He had shot the horses, and to see such fine animals destroyed by his bullets was a terrible thing to behold. Yet he had been caught up in the moment and after his first shot, he did not think, did not try to balance death with what he knew of life. He had just done what Schneck told him to do, and it was like shooting elk at first when he could only see the hairy hides and not the entire target.

It was only after he saw the horses go down and saw the blood that he felt the pangs of regret course through his body. And when Sweeney had shot the two outriders, he hadn't felt any remorse. Instead, he had put mental distance between him and the two riders as they had been torn from their saddles by the force of rifle bullets. They had seemed like large mannequins pulled from their mounts by an invisible string. He had not felt anything. Those men were foreigners. They were sheepherders. They were his mortal enemies.

The first child had been a small boy. Jackson had seen him jump from the second wagon and run straight toward him. He yelled words in a language LouDon did not understand, but he thought he recognized the word "mama" just before he squeezed the trigger, felt his rifle buck against his shoulder, and saw the bullet smash into the little boy's chest just below his young throat.

The boy had collapsed in a tumbling heap, arms and legs flailing wildly, blood gushing onto the ground and soaking into the sand and gravel. LouDon squinched his eyes until they were almost shut, but the pandemonium incited him to pick out other targets and swing his rifle barrel to pick them up, one by one, lever another cartridge into the firing chamber, and squeeze the trigger when his front sight, the muzzle of his rifle, picked up the figure and blotted it out just before he fired his gun.

It was carnage he realized now. None of those women and children had a chance in hell of escaping the slaughter.

He had been a part of it, and now he could not get the
pictures of those innocent little kids out of his mind. He was
sick beyond sickness, and his empty stomach was now raw
and twitching as if it had been scoured with iron files, the
lining scraped clean and left to fester. He knew he had to get
out of there before they spotted him. He turned his horse and
let the animal creep away a step at a time so it would not
make too much noise. He headed for some place deeper into
the timber, away from the road. He looked over his shoulder
and listened to the soft voices of the two men until they either
stopped or faded in the distance between him and them.

He had not traveled more than a hundred yards or so when
he heard a noise behind him.

He could not see well through the myriad of pine trees and
spruce trees, the white scarred trunks of the aspens, but he
knew someone was following him. He resisted the urge to
bury his spurs in his horse's flanks and ride away at high
speed. Some instinct told him to go slow and perhaps he
could slink away into the forest and get the hell out of there
without being seen.

He patted his horse on the neck and leaned over the saddle horn so that he had some protection from a bullet in the
back.

Then he heard the voice from behind him, and his blood
froze.

"Where you goin', LouDon?"

LouDon recognized the voice. He sat up straight and
turned around.

There, riding through the trees at a slow pace, was a man
he knew, a man he did not want to know he had seen with the
Sidewinder.

He pretended not to know and let out a sign of relief.

"Howdy, Thor," LouDon said as he hauled in on the reins
and stopped his horse. "What in hell are you doin' way out
here?"

Sorenson kept coming toward him. Closer and closer.

"I might ask you the same thing, LouDon. You're pretty far from camp, aren't you?"

Jackson felt trapped, but what could he do?

"Me'n Sweeney, Jim, and Otto rode down here in the middle of the night. We been here all mornin'."

Sorenson rode still closer, steady and slow.

"I don't see nobody but you here, LouDon."

"Oh, they all headed back to camp. Left me here for a time. Did you see what we done out there on the road?"

"I sure did," Sorenson drawled. There was no rancor in his voice, no sign that he either approved or disapproved. His voice was just flat and tinged with that Minnesota-Swedish accent.

"Hell of a mess, ain't it? But we sure taught them sheepherders a lesson, by God."

"Yeah, looks like you did."

"Schneck thinks them herders will pull out with their sheep as soon as word gets back to 'em what we all did."

Sorenson rode to within ten feet of Jackson and halted his horse. He just sat there, resting both overlapped hands on his saddle horn. It was like the two of them had met out in the middle of a pasture and were just jawing with each other real friendly-like. At least that's the way LouDon pictured their meeting. Just a couple of men chewing the fat over the weather or maybe complaining about the hard life of a cowpoke. At least he hoped he could convince Sorenson that it was okay to do what they had done.

"Yeah, LouDon, could be. That's what I would do if I saw what you fellers did to all those women and kids."

"I think one of the women got away," LouDon said. "I seen her run off into the woods, but I didn't get a chance to pull down on her. Hell, she's probably clean gone to Texas by now."

"Gone to Texas?"

"Oh, that's just an expression. Means she lit a shuck. Took a powder. Plumb run off somewhere."

"She the only one who got away?"

"I reckon. Hell, things was happenin' so fast, I couldn't keep track of it all."

"That must have been something," Sorenson said in that smooth, even voice of his.

"You shoulda seen it, Thor. It was a sight, I tell you."

"I'll bet it was," Sorenson said.

"Say, who's with you? I thought I heard a couple of voices. Ned? Percy?"

"Nope," Sorenson said. "Neither of them."

"Who, then?"

"I don't think you know the man, LouDon. Folks hereabouts call him 'Sidewinder.'"

"Sidewinder? The one that killed our guys?"

"I reckon. He's a detective from Denver. Raises cattle, too."

"A detective?"

"Yeah. He's the man who killed Grunewald. Outdrawed him and shot him plumb dead."

Jackson's face drained all its pink and tan, as if his veins had been flushed full of white paint. He swallowed so that his Adam's apple bobbed and tautened the skin on his throat.

"What're you doin' with him, Thor?" Jackson's voice was a squeak coming out of that tight throat of his.

"Oh, I'm working for him, LouDon. He done hired me as a detective. We both work for that detective agency in Denver. We're helping out the sheepherders, trying to find Schneck and put him in jail so he can get himself hanged."

"You sonofabitch," LouDon said as the realization hit that he could not get away.

At the same time, LouDon grabbed for his pistol.

Sorenson smiled wanly and jerked his own pistol from its holster.

He was a tad slower than LouDon, but he was more deliberate.

LouDon cleared leather and thumbed the hammer back.

Sorenson prodded his horse forward with a light tick of his spurs in both flanks.

LouDon raised his arm and took aim at Sorenson.

Sorenson's horse kept coming. He peeled back the hammer of his Colt as LouDon squeezed the trigger.

Sorenson ducked and heard the whine of the bullet as it whizzed over his head.

He brought up his pistol and squeezed the trigger within five feet of LouDon.

LouDon jerked on his reins with his left hand and tried to turn his horse and gallop away.

Sorenson's bullet struck him in his left side, just under his armpit.

LouDon felt the jolt of the impact, but he felt no pain. Instead, he felt a rush of heat and blood to his head, and a dizziness assailed him.

He half turned in the saddle and raised his arm to shoot at Sorenson again.

The trees around LouDon turned fuzzy, and Sorenson turned into a liquid shadow that shimmered like some kind of strange mirage, his body all wavery and misty, out of focus.

Then the pain hit him.

LouDon felt as if fire had entered his body, as if someone had shoved a hot, cherry-red poker into his side, and he heard something wheeze inside of him, as if one of his lungs had collapsed and spewed out part of his breath. The pain was so great that he closed his eyes.

His pistol fell from his hand, and the sound of it striking the ground was far away, muffled, as if it had fallen into a thick comforter or into another dimension. None of it made any sense to LouDon. Nothing was right. The tall pines spun around him when he opened his eyes, and the sky blurred into a gray-black smear of nothingness, emptiness.

He opened his mouth, but it was just a reflex. He could not find any air to breathe. No air came out, no oxygen came in.

He felt as if he was being blotted out, smashed like a bug on a tabletop, squashed dead under Sorenson's boot.

His horse stopped, and LouDon fell to the ground.

Sorenson looked down at Jackson's body.

He felt nothing.

LouDon was just a hired hand. Schneck had put him up to the massacre of all those women and children.

Schneck was the man who should have been lying there dead on the ground.

Sorenson drew in a deep breath and turned his horse. He looked at the sky, the bulging bellies of the black clouds.

But he knew it wasn't going to rain.

The wind blew hard, and he knew that it was going to be cold.

And where, he wondered, had Schneck, Sweeney, and Wagner gone in this mountain wilderness where there were so many places to hide and so many places to kill?

"One down," he said to himself. "And three to go."

TWENTY-FIVE

∽

The three riders heard the two pistol shots as they wended their way through the timber, heading for the ford they had crossed earlier that day. All three men halted their horses and looked back toward the dying and distorted sound.

"Did you hear that, Boss?" Sweeney said to Schneck.

"Yeah, we all heard it, Sweeney," Schneck said, a sarcastic tone to his voice. "Do you think we're deaf?"

Sweeney looked ashamed and did not answer.

"Sounded like pistol shots," Wagner said. "Back there where we come from."

"Listen," Schneck said, waving the other two men to silence.

They heard the breathing of their horses and the swishing sound as they swished their tails.

The shots echoed off the rocky outcroppings and died in the hush of the forest. The low, black-bottomed clouds seemed to soak up the sounds as they drifted overhead.

"It's awful quiet," Wagner whispered loud enough for Schneck and Sweeney to hear him.

"Yeah," Sweeney breathed as he twisted his head as if to pick up any voice calling out for help.

"Just shut up," Schneck said, irritated.

Several moments passed with none of the men saying anything.

"I don't hear nothin' else," Wagner said.

"No," Schneck agreed.

"You told LouDon to fire two shots if he got in trouble, Boss," Sweeney ventured.

"I know what I said, Halbert, you fool," Schneck snapped.

"We better get back there," Wagner said.

Schneck drew in a breath. His neck began to swell with anger, and his lips twisted so that his expression took on a sour look.

"Yeah," Schneck said, finally, "we better get back there and see what's up."

"Those were sure as hell pistol shots," Sweeney said.

"But who was doin' the shootin'?" Wagner asked.

"Sounded like LouDon," Sweeney replied.

"I wish you two would just shut up," Schneck said. "I'm trying to think. Those shots might have been fired off by Jackson, but maybe whoever came down that road was shooting at him. We just don't know."

"No," Wagner said, "I reckon we don't. Not for sure, anyways."

The men turned their horses and began to pick their way back toward the place where they had left Jackson. Every so often, Schneck stopped them to listen, but they heard nothing.

Schneck was suspicious of the two shots. An uneasy feeling came over him.

There should have been more shots, he thought. After those first two. What kind of trouble was Jackson in? Had he just fired his pistols into the air, or had he shot at somebody?

If he had shot at someone, then he killed either one or two men. If he had missed, then there should have been at least one answering shot. But they had heard only two shots.

If Jackson had fired his pistol because he was in trouble, where was he? He knew where they were going, and he should be riding toward them. But there was no sound of hoofbeats, no sound of a horse running through the timber, crashing through brush.

He thought it was very strange that they had heard only those two shots.

And there was no certainty that Jackson had been the one who fired his pistol.

"Let's not be in a hurry," Schneck said to Wagner. "We have no way of knowing what we're getting into."

"I agree," Wagner said.

They rode slowly and they stopped to listen every few minutes.

The silence was almost unbearable to all three men.

A half hour later, with Wagner in the lead, Sweeney right behind him, and Schneck bringing up the rear as they rode single file, they all heard sounds from somewhere ahead of them.

Voices. Men's voices.

They halted, then lined up side by side to try and decipher the voices.

They were quiet for several moments.

"Hey, ain't that the Swede's voice?" Sweeney said.

"Maybe, yeah," Wagner said. "Sure sounds like the Swede."

Schneck cupped a hand to his ear. He stood up in his stirrups as if to hear better.

The voices sounded closer.

"I think that might be Sorenson," Schneck said. "What in hell is he doin' down here?"

"Who's that with him?" Sweeney asked. "That other voice don't sound familiar at all."

"I don't like this a damned bit," Schneck said. "Halbert,

you'd better ride over yonder real slow and find out what the hell's going on. And see who in hell is with Sorenson, because that's his voice, sure as I'm sitting here."

Sweeney looked at Schneck. "Me?" he said.

"Yeah, you, Sweeney," Schneck said.

"We'll be right behind you," Wagner said.

But neither he nor Schneck moved their horses as Sweeney reluctantly headed for the road.

Sweeney was shivering all over, and it wasn't from the chill wind that was blowing through the timber and pushing all the clouds toward the east. He drew his pistol and looked back at Schneck and Wagner, neither of whom had moved an inch.

Wagner moved his hand in a signal for Sweeney to keep going.

Sweeney kept going, and the wind began to keen in the treetops. He wound through the pines at a slow clip.

Ahead, he glimpsed two men on horseback. One of them he recognized as Sorenson.

There was a man he had never seen before, and he was leading a horse he had seen before and knew.

It was LouDon's horse.

And the saddle was empty.

TWENTY-SIX

∿

Brad followed Sorenson to the place where he had shot Jackson.

"He's dead, all right," he said. "I'm going to take his horse with us. We have to find Vivelda. She's somewhere in this timber. She's either running or she's hiding out."

"I agree," Sorenson said. "We've got to find that girl before Schneck hunts her down."

"You might want to strip the dead man of his pistol and knife. Put them in the saddlebags."

"Yeah, I'll do that," Sorenson said.

He dismounted and walked over to Jackson's body. He unbuckled his pistol belt and picked his gun off the ground and jammed it back in its holster. The knife was attached to the belt. He rolled the leather up and stuffed them in one of Jackson's saddlebags, then mounted his horse.

"A lot of burying to do, Brad. Him and the others."

"We may have to let this one ripen for a few days. If we

can find Vivelda, she can ride this horse back up and tell them all what happened here."

"By herself?" Sorenson asked.

"No, you are going with her, Thor. Make sure she gets back all right."

"But what about Schneck and the two other men, Wagner and Sweeney?"

"That's only three against one."

"Not good odds, you ask me."

"I've had worse," Brad said.

They both heard a noise off to their left and reined up their horses.

"What was that?" Brad said.

"I don't know," Sorenson replied.

They both looked off into the timber. Brad saw a horse's legs through the trees. He wheeled Ginger around and held out the reins of Jackson's horse to Sorenson. "Here, hold on to the horse while I take a look," Brad said.

Sorenson grabbed the reins. He couldn't see what Brad had been looking at, so he just held his horse there and watched as Brad rode a few yards and ducked low over his saddle horn.

Brad pulled on the leather thong around his neck and brought the set of rattles into his hand. He held them at his side in his left hand as he rode in a zigzag pattern toward the animal he had spotted.

Through the trees, he saw the man sitting his horse. He seemed to be looking toward the road and listening.

Brad rode in close and quiet.

Ginger's hoof dislodged a stone, and the iron made a scraping noise as it grazed the loose rock.

The man on the horse jerked his head in the direction of the sound, but Brad rode behind a pair of trees.

"That you, Sorenson?" Sweeney called out.

Brad did not answer.

Instead, he shook the rattles. He shook them loud and

long. The man on the horse jerked upright in his saddle and swung his pistol toward the ground.

To Brad's surprise, the sound brought a rattlesnake out of hiding beneath a large flat rock. It slithered into view and then raised its tail and began to shake it so that the dozen or so rattles replicated the sound of his own.

The man on the horse became fully visible. Brad saw him staring at the ground and scanning back and forth to locate the rattlesnake.

Brad rode on past the snake and let his own rattles fall from his hand and dangle at the end of the looped thong.

Sweeney saw Brad emerge from behind a small fir tree and swung his pistol.

"Hey, you," Sweeney said.

"You cock that pistol and it's the last thing you'll do," Brad said, his right hand floating above his pistol butt like a hovering hawk.

"Huh?" Sweeney said.

"Drop the gun," Brad said in a quiet, even tone.

The snake ceased its rattling behind Brad, but he could hear it wriggle though the dried pine needles as it slithered away.

"You go to hell," Sweeney said. He raised his arm and pressed his thumb down on the hammer. There was a distinct click as the hammer locked into full cock.

Brad's hand was a blur as he jerked his Colt from its holster, cocking the hammer back as he leveled the barrel at Sweeney from his hip. He squeezed the trigger and felt the jolt of the pistol as the cartridge exploded and whirred through the grooves of the barrel. The lead spun in a spiral and left the muzzle at a high rate of speed.

With unerring accuracy, the bullet smacked into Sweeney's breastbone, splitting it apart, ripping through a lung, and tearing a hole the size of a quarter in his back as it traveled through flesh, veins, and muscle.

Sweeney's finger was on the trigger, but he could not

squeeze it. All feeling went out of his hand, and his pistol fell from limp, rubbery fingers. The gun hit the ground, butt first, and toppled over.

Brad brought his pistol up to shoulder level and took aim for a second shot.

Sweeney's eyes slanted askew. His mouth opened in an O of surprise. Pain swarmed through his chest like a cloud of fire, and tears stung his eyes.

He gasped out a sound and then slumped over as a plume of blood spurted from the hole in his chest, thick and rich with oxygen. A spasm convulsed his upper torso, and more blood poured from the hole in his back as wine from a spout.

Brad did not squeeze off a second shot. It was unnecessary. He watched as the man crumpled and fell over his saddle horn, his feet still caught firmly in his stirrups. The horse beneath him took a step and then stood stock-still.

Sweeney's breath was a quiet rasp in his throat, a mere reflex in a mortally wounded man. One of Sweeney's legs jerked, and then he stopped breathing. A last gust of air escaped from his lungs and did not return.

Brad sat there for a moment, then slipped the rattles back inside his shirt. He opened the gate on his cylinder, set the hammer at half cock and spun the magazine until he saw the dimpled firing pin. He pulled the ramrod down and ejected the spent shell. He slid a fresh one from his belt into the empty channel and then closed the gate, moved the cylinder so that the hammer would fall in between and shoved his pistol back in his holster.

"Get him?" Sorenson called.

"Yeah," Brad answered and turned his horse in a half circle.

He rode back to where Sorenson was waiting for him.

"Two down," he said. "Two to go."

"Let me see who it was," Sorenson said. "You hold the reins while I take a quick look."

Brad waited until Sorenson returned, then headed north to look for Vivelda.

"That was Halbert Sweeney you shot," he said. "That means that Schneck and Wagner are somewhere close by or else riding away hell-bent for leather."

"Let's find that girl and I'll see if I can't pick up the tracks of those two," Brad said.

"Well, you're lessening the odds some," Sorenson said. "Now it's only two against two."

"Good odds," Brad said, but he kept looking over his shoulder as the two scoured the underbrush, looking for Vivelda.

"Sweeney's slumped over his saddle," Sorenson said. "Maybe the horse will carry him back to the cow camp for all to see."

"I reckon if that horse climbs these slopes, Sweeney will fall off somewhere, and the buzzards and the worms and the coyotes will have them a feast."

Sorenson said nothing.

A moment later, Brad jerked up straight in the saddle and pointed ahead.

"What is it?" Sorenson said.

"I saw something, I think."

"What? Where?"

"Up in those gray rocks, off to the left. Something."

The two men rode closer to a jumble of rocks that seemed to grow out of the earth.

"Vivelda," Brad called. "It's me, Brad Storm. You're safe now. Come out."

He stopped his horse and listened. Sorenson did the same.

There was only silence as the wind blew against their clothes and moved the clouds faster out over the foothills and the long prairie.

The wind moaned in the hollows and crevices of the rocks.

Brad thought it was the loneliest sound in the world as he felt the chill bumps rise on his arms and crawl up his neck like a thousand icy spiders.

TWENTY-SEVEN

᭯

Wagner and Schneck both jerked upright in their saddles when they heard the single pistol shot. It was unexpected and came from the direction where Sweeney had ridden to check on Sorenson.

The two men looked at each other. Wagner shrugged. Schneck scowled.

"You don't think Sorenson shot Halbert, do you, Otto? It did sound like Sorenson earlier."

"Or do I think Sweeney shot Sorenson, you mean?"

"Could have gone either way, I reckon. Maybe Sweeney rode up on Sorenson and, with all them bodies lyin' there, Sorenson might have thought he was next."

"So, you think maybe Sorenson shot Sweeney?" Schneck said.

"I ain't sayin' that, Otto."

"No, you're not saying much. But we'd better check. Something's sure as hell cockeyed here, and I mean to get to the bottom of it."

"Sure, Boss. You want me to ride out there and take a look-see?"

Schneck considered that offer for a second or two and shook his head.

"No," he said, "we'll both ride out there and see what's going on. I'm just as curious as you, Jim."

The two rode in tandem toward the road. Schneck pulled his rifle from his boot and laid it across the pommel of his saddle at an angle. Wagner hesitated as he reached for his own rifle but left it in his scabbard.

"Seems to me you're mighty confident, Jim. Leaving your rifle in its boot."

"I ain't confident at all, Otto. I just want both hands free in case we have to get the hell away."

"Away from what?"

"Hell, we don't know. What if it is Sorenson, and if it is, what's he doin' down here? Or who's with him? Maybe he joined up with them sheepherders."

"Jim, you ought to do something about that wild imagination of yours. Why would Sorenson join up with the sheepherders? They're our enemy."

"I don't know. Might be they made him a better offer, Otto."

"You're full of shit, Jim. Sorenson wouldn't just ride down to the sheepherders' camp and ask for a job."

"No, I reckon he wouldn't. Maybe I am full of shit."

They spoke no more until they saw Sweeney's horse standing hipshot a few yards in front of them.

Only the rump of the horse was showing until they rode up alongside and saw Sweeney slumped over the saddle. His pistol lay on the ground next to the horse, a dim light from the cloudy sky streaming across the bluing of the barrel.

"Hey, Halbert," Wagner said, "you sleepin' on the job?"

He reached out to touch Sweeney on the shoulder, then saw the black and tattered hole with bits of bloody wool around it as if something had gouged his well-lined jacket with a pruning fork. The hole in his back was the size of a two-bit piece. Wagner withdrew his hand with lightning speed, as if he had touched a finger to an open flame.

"Jesus," Wagner said. "He's dead."

Schneck picked up his rifle and waved the barrel in a small arc as if expecting to be attacked at any minute.

"Shot in the back," Schneck said as he glanced over at Sweeney.

"Nope. He was shot in the front. That's a damned exit hole, Otto."

"So, Sweeney's dead," Schneck said, as if he were speaking to himself in order to make it final.

Wagner looked at Schneck as if he thought his boss had become addled all of a sudden. The look on Schneck's face was blank. The German had no expression whatsoever. It was as if an unseen hand had wiped all semblance of humanity from his features and left a waxen image in its place.

Wagner got an uneasy feeling just then.

The Schneck he had known up until that day had been strong and resolute. Now he looked washed out and washed up, as if some force had cleaned him out and left a lifeless hulk in his place. It was just a feeling, but that one glimpse had begun to shatter Wagner's confidence that he was working for a man who was always in control.

"Get his guns and let's go after whoever shot Sweeney," Schneck said, his voice devoid of any feeling.

"What?" Wagner said, as if the request had left him in shock.

"You heard me. Grab his pistol and rifle. We got to hunt down the man who shot Sweeney."

"Christ, Boss, I don't want his guns."

"I do. We can sell them if nothing else."

"You get 'em, then, Otto. I ain't touchin' nothin' of Halbert's, and that's that."

Schneck fixed him with dagger of a look, but only his eyes

betrayed his anger at being countermanded. His face was like a cold pudding.

"I'll send someone down for his horse."

"And to bury him," Wagner said.

"I don't care about that," Schneck said. "Leave him to the buzzards for all I care. The dumb sonofabitch."

Wagner said nothing.

He followed Schneck as he rode toward the road. As they left the place where they had found Sweeney's body, they both heard a warning rattle and saw a timber rattler coil up next to a downed tree. Its tongue streaked in and out of his mouth like black lightning with twin forks.

"Kind of early for rattlers," Wagner said as he circled away from the snake.

Schneck gave him a dirty look.

"I don't want to hear about rattlesnakes," he said.

Wagner sighed and let it go. Something inside Schneck had changed. He wasn't the same man Wagner had known for the past two years or so. Yet, he seemed determined to find the man who had killed Sweeney. It just seemed as if all the fire had gone out of him, and he was just going through the motions, like a soldier that has killed his first man, lost his mind, and just keeps marching forward, shooting at anything that moves.

Wagner stayed a few yards behind Schneck as they reached the road, and both looked at all the dead bodies of men, horses, women, and children. It was a sickening sight now that he could see the lifeless bodies and remember that they had once been alive and happy, laughing and talking until the gunfire broke out and they began to scream just before they died in a hail of bullets.

He didn't like what he had done. He knew, deep down in his heart, that he would never get over any of it. And now, seeing all the dead, it was worse. The images of before and after were seared in his mind for as long as he lived.

"Let's track them," Schneck said in that same toneless voice.

"Yes, sir, I'll try," Wagner said and took the lead. He scanned the ground and sorted out the tracks. He saw where one horse had gone into the woods and returned from where Sweeney had been killed. Then that horse joined up with another and both had ridden into the timber where they would be harder to track.

That took him better than a half hour, while Schneck sat there with his rifle butt resting on his leg, staring up at the windblown clouds and the blue, green, and silver waters of the river crashing down through the long canyon on its rush to the South Platte. He gazed up at the high mountains and seemed impervious to the brisk and gusting wind that coursed down on them like some icebound reminder of winter and an unsettled spring.

"It's going to be slow goin' through them trees," Wagner said.

"I don't care how long it takes," Schneck said. "I'm going to kill the man who shot Sweeney."

"There are two men down here in the timber," Wagner said.

"I'll kill both of them. One of them is probably that goddamned detective."

"Probably," Wagner said. Then, to push the needle deeper into Schneck, he added, "The one they call Sidewinder."

He saw Schneck stiffen as if he had been knifed in the back, and it gave him a perverse satisfaction for some reason.

"You ain't so damned big, Schneck," he said to himself. "You're probably just as scared as me about that Sidewinder feller."

And Wagner was scared. The man they called Sidewinder was an unknown factor in all this sheepherder business. He was a man that Schneck didn't know and couldn't kill so easy as women and kids. He'd bet his bottom dollar that Schneck was scared, too.

He just wouldn't admit it to nobody.

Because, down deep, Schneck was a born killer, and he had no heart. Or, if he did have one, it was made of iron and pumped poison instead of blood.

He was sorry now that he even knew Otto Schneck.

But he did know him. He knew Schneck too damned well.

TWENTY-EIGHT

∽

Vivelda ran as she had never run before, with a flaming ball of terror blazing in her mind, a terror so alien to her that she could not connect any part of it to the real world, the world of childhood and young womanhood that she had known when she was nurtured in the comforting arms of her mother, Imelda Udaberri, and the deep calm voice of her father, Alberto. She had never known a terror such as the one that burned her thoughts to a crisp like crumpled pieces of paper tossed into an open fire.

Reason deserted her as she ran, headlong, through a strange and terrifying wilderness where branches grabbed at her blouse and her skirt like the fingers of skeletons, and stones bruised her bare feet, brush scratched her ankles and legs like the raking claws of feral cats. Every crashing sound of her feet sent new alarms through her brain with the speed and heat of electric energy. She wanted to scream, but her throat was constricted and her brain burning up with the horror of what she had witnessed and could not process. Her mind was filled with the screams of children and the terrified shouts of her friends and the terrible sight of horses falling dead in their traces, men she knew toppling from their horses with blood spurting from their bodies like red wine from a shattered goatskin *la bota*, and the crack of the rifles like the sound of dry bones breaking under the hammer blows of hidden monsters.

She ran and stumbled and fell. She scraped her knees on sharp stones and desiccated branches. She picked herself up and rubbed the fresh red scars on her legs, then careened on, climbing steep terrain and falling into ditches and treacherous depressions in the earth that added to her terror.

She felt sure that men were chasing her. Men with rifles and knives. She could hear them in her mind, their heavy boots smashing downed branches and crushing rocks to powder. She did not look back because that would ignite more fires of that terror that burned all through her, frying her brain, paralyzing her heart, and searing her tired legs so that they ached with muscle cramps that felt like a fist was squeezing them so hard that she was sure they would give out on her and she would fall and never get up.

Sounds and voices faded away, and she ran and tripped in silence. Her chest burned with the agony of a long-distance runner. When she saw the large cairn of rocks ahead of her, jutting out of a short slope, she staggered toward it, breathing hard. There were crevices and crawl spaces among the gray boulders, and she knew she had to rest. And hide.

In the thin air, she was starved for oxygen. Her muscles began to tighten up on her, and she had cramps in both of her calves. Her feet were sore and tender from the hard rocks underfoot.

Vivelda clambered up to the stack of large stones. She bent over and extended her hand to one of the lower ones, bracing herself as she struggled to breathe. It took several minutes before she could breathe normally and without that searing pain in her lungs. She glanced back down the slope to see if anyone had followed her. She was relieved to see no

one there. She looked up at the formidable array of rocks.
They looked like a stone altar in the shape of a lumpy pyra-
mid, somehow comforting, as if it might be some way station
for weary huntsmen in the deep woods. She walked around
to the other side and saw a crevice large enough for her to
crawl into and rest for a spell.

She stooped down and peered into the dark hole amid the
rocks. She looked for animal tracks in the soft earth but saw
nothing but dried brown pine needles blown there by a long
ago wind. She squatted down and felt the ground inside. It
was dry against the palm of her hand. She breathed a sigh of
relief and, on hands and knees, crawled inside. The hole was
just big enough so that she could turn around and sit if she
hunched over and pulled her legs up close to her chest.

She nestled against a rock at her back and sat scrunched
up like some woodland creature peering out into the shadowy
landscape flocked with pines and spruce, a couple of alder
thickets. She could hear the river as it cascaded down the
canyon. She rested her head on the tops of her skinned-up
knees and closed her eyes for a few seconds. She heard her
heart pounding in her chest, and it sounded loud to her, but
regular as her breathing had become. The clouds across the
river seemed low enough to touch, almost, and they were dark
and bulging with stored-up rain.

A few moments later, she heard voices in the distance.
She shuddered in fear and pressed against the rock behind
her as if to conceal herself even more from anyone who might
pass by and look for her in her hiding place.

The voices grew louder as she knew someone was getting
closer to where she was hiding. She listened and her heart
pumped faster. The fear in her mind flared up and made her
tremble as if gripped by a sudden chill. She closed her eyes
and prayed to the Holy Mother Mary.

"Don't let them find me and kill me," she added in the
silence of her mind. "Please don't let them find me."

She stifled a sob as the voices grew still louder. Men's voices. Very close.

Her heart seemed to skip a beat when she saw the legs of the horses, and a half second later, the figures of two men. They seemed to be following her tracks, because they both looked down at the ground as they rode very slowly straight to the place where she had climbed up to the rocky cairn.

Then, she heard one of them call her name.

"Vivelda. It's me, Brad Storm. You're safe now."

She saw the man who had spoken and recognized him. It was Brad, but who was the man with him? Was he one of those who had shot her friends and killed them? She had never seen that man before. He was leading a horse behind him, a horse with an empty saddle. So she didn't move.

She watched as Brad dismounted and walked toward her. She whimpered as she saw him looking at the ground and circling the pile of rocks. He stopped in front of the opening and bent over.

"Vivelda, are you in there?" he asked.

She whimpered but could not speak.

"It's all right. The man with me is a friend and he is going to take you back to Mikel."

Brad held out his hand.

"I can't see you," he said, "but I know you're in there. Come on out. We have a horse for you to ride. You'll be safe with this man. He will take you back up to the valley where Mikel and Joe will take care of you."

She squealed and crawled out of the hole. She scrambled on her hands and knees to where Brad stood hunched over and reached out to him with her left hand. He grasped it and pulled her to her feet. Then he drew her to him and enfolded her in his arms.

He patted the back of her head as she sobbed uncontrollably against the warmth of his chest, the rough hide of the buckskin.

"There, there," he said softly. "You're going to be all right. You will be safe from those bad men."

"Oh, Brad," she sobbed, "I am so happy to see you."

Then she laughed hysterically as he led her by the hand down to the horses.

"Vivelda, this is Thor. He works for me. You can trust him. Can you ride?"

She nodded dumbly and looked up at Sorenson.

"I—I can ride," she said.

Brad helped her into the saddle of the horse next to Sorenson. He adjusted the stirrup straps as he poked her left foot into one of them. Then he walked around to the other side and worked the straps until she could rest her foot on the rung. She looked down at him in gratitude.

"You'll be home in no time," he said.

"Am I—am I the only one?"

"Yes," Brad said. "I'm so sorry. I'll get the men who did that."

Then he looked up at Sorenson. "Thor, take her home."

"I will," Sorenson said. "Just follow me, little lady. I'll hold on to the reins. You just hold on to that saddle horn."

Vivelda nodded, and fresh tears streamed down from her eyes onto her cheeks. She grabbed the saddle horn with both hands, and Thor clucked to his horse and tapped his spurs into its flanks.

Brad waved to them as they rode off, back up the canyon, along the road that bordered the Poudre. Soon, the two were out of sight, and he let out a long breath of relief.

He led Ginger up behind the jumble of rocks and kept going until he found a small clearing that was concealed by some junipers, spruces, and several pines. He ground-tied his horse to a low sturdy young juniper. He dug into a saddlebag and grabbed a box of .30-caliber cartridges and a handful of double-ought shot shells. He pulled his rifle from its scabbard, walked around, and slipped the shotgun off his saddle horn. He walked back down the slope and climbed the backside of the rocks. He sat there on the top rock with a pine tree at his back. The rock was large enough so that he could lay the shotgun down. He leaned against the tree and jacked a cartridge into the firing chamber of the Winchester.

He looked down at the road, which was some distance away. Then he marked the place where he and Sorenson had stopped. If anyone was following them, that was where they would end up, at that spot where Vivelda had climbed up the slope and found her hiding place.

He wasn't sure that Schneck and Wagner would follow Vivelda's tracks, overlaid with his and Sorenson's horse-shoe impressions, but if they did come along, he was ready for them.

A gray squirrel skittered down from a tree and prowled the earth below him, searching for nuggets of food among the fallen pinecones. A chipmunk dashed across his line of vision, its nervous tail stiff and upright and twitching at every pause in its tiny journey down to the river. He heard it squeal just before it dove into a hole among the rocks along the shore.

Brad waited for what seemed a long time, but he knew was less than an hour. He was watching the clouds and knew the sun was on its descending arc. The clouds were finally thinning, and some of those he saw were ivory white and carried no hint of rain. Beyond these, he saw patches of blue sky and a snow-clad mountain peak rising like some majestic monument behind the shadowy ridges arrayed in dim phalanxes far beyond the canyon.

He stretched his legs and wiggled his toes inside his boots. He was about to get up and walk back to where Ginger was tethered when he heard the soft snort of a horse and the muffled sound of hooves striking the ground, rustling in the brush.

Brad scooted around and lay flat on the large rock. There, he could see without being seen. The tree at his back served to block his silhouette. He took off his hat and laid it next to the Greener, still in its case.

He hoped he would not need the shotgun.

Two men appeared atop horses. The one in front was studying the ground as he rode. The man behind him had his rifle resting across his lap. He held his reins with his left hand while his right hand rested on the receiver of the rifle.

Brad took the man in front to be the foreman, Jim Wagner. The man riding behind him had to be Otto Schneck.

Brad touched the pine with his boot and braced himself as he brought his rifle stock up against his cheek and nestled the butt against his shoulder.

Wagner stopped and held up a hand to Schneck.

"Stay there, while I look around," Wagner said in a low voice. "Somethin' ain't right here."

Schneck reined up and sat there, looking around him. He picked up his rifle and rested the butt on his leg while his fingers slipped inside the lever except for his thumb and index finger. His finger slid inside the trigger guard, and his thumb braced the stock.

Schneck stared up at the tower of rocks. He seemed to be staring straight at Brad.

Brad did not move and held his breath while his eyes moved in their sockets, and he stared at Wagner.

Wagner rode a few yards ahead and then walked his horse in a circle as he deciphered the maze of tracks.

Brad could almost hear what the man was thinking. He was thinking as Brad would if he were studying the tracks. Three horses, the small footprints of Vivelda, his own boot tracks. Tracks coming and going up to the pile of boulders.

Then, two horses leaving, heading for the road along the Poudre. Then, more boot tracks and one horse leaving its spoor alongside the walking man.

Wagner finished his assessment and interpretation of the tracks and looked up at the brazen cairn of rocks, like a small citadel in the forest. He studied them for several seconds.

Brad eased back the hammer of his rifle while holding the trigger and pulling it slightly so that the snick of the hammer was muffled. He cocked the rifle. There was a small sound, a slight metallic click as he brought the hammer back to full cock with his thumb.

Wagner seemed to twitch slightly at the sound, but instead of drawing his rifle from its boot or drawing his pistol, he turned his horse and rode back to where Schneck was waiting.

He said something to Schneck, but Brad could not hear it. Nor did Schneck betray the message by staring up at the rocks.

Instead, Schneck slipped out of his saddle on the right side. Wagner pulled his rifle from its scabbard and almost dove out of his saddle. He whopped his horse on the rump while Schneck took up a position behind an aspen tree. The snout of his barrel edged around the white trunk.

Wagner slapped the rump of Schneck's horse and then jumped behind a stately pine.

Brad heard the cartridge set in the firing chamber as Wagner worked the lever of his rifle up and down.

Could they see him atop the rocks? Brad wondered.

In the sudden hush, Brad could hear his heart thump in measured beats. He took in a breath and held it, his finger on the rifle trigger.

Seconds of pure silence passed by, and the last white clouds floated past. Sunlight streamed down onto the river and painted its waters golden and crimson.

The first shot shattered the silence. White smoke billowed from Wagner's rifle, and the air danced with motes of flame. The bullet whined a keening song as it sped straight toward the rock where Brad lay flat as a lizard hiding from a flying hawk.

The crack of the rifle echoed up and down the canyon.

The sound seemed to last an eternity, like the distant sound of an ocean in a seashell.

TWENTY-NINE

෨

Brad's hat took flight and sailed off like a thrown discus into the trees behind him. The bullet grazed the rock as it caught the brim, spewing a small shower of sparks as it caromed into the pine behind Brad with a resounding smack and splintered pine bark and wood pulp until it came to a stop in the shape of a leaden mushroom.

He had no clear shot at either man, but Brad knew he had to keep them pinned down or either one might shoot him off the rock. He fired a round at Schneck and saw the bullet rip off a chunk of tree bark just above the cattleman's head. He swung his rifle to bear on Wagner, levered another cartridge into the firing chamber, and squeezed off a shot. The bullet thunked into the tree concealing Wagner, and Brad saw him pull the exposed part of his body to full concealment by standing sideways.

He scooted backward, sliding his boot off the tree behind the rock as both men fired at him. He saw the flame and heard the bullets smack into the rock, then ricochet off at an angle with a high-pitched whine. The two men kept firing at him so fast that he had to hold his head down and shove himself backward until his boots touched soft ground on the slope.

Brad fired off another round that he knew was too high, but he heard it strike the tree where Schneck stood.

Both Schneck and Wagner kept firing their rifles, levering so fast that their aim was poor. Their bullets struck the rock, showering Brad with stinging sparks and chipping large chunks of rock away as they sailed off into the timber like whirring hornets. They kept firing until their rifles were empty, and Brad heard them as they jammed fresh cartridges into their magazines.

He used the delay to back down even farther behind the pile of rocks until he was on solid ground. He worked his way around the rock pile, keeping his head down, until he had a clear view of both trees and flashes of arms and legs. He fired off two quick shots from his rifle, one at each tree, and heard Wagner curse as his face or arm was stung by flying bark.

Brad jacked another cartridge into the firing chamber of his Winchester but did not shoot. Instead he hugged the ground and listened to bullets scream over his head or chip away at the rocks. The two men kept firing, and bullets whistled over Brad's head like angry bees.

The firing stopped, and Brad heard Wagner call out to Schneck.

"I'm out of bullets, Otto. How about you?"

"About two or three shots left," Schneck growled.

Brad snaked the barrel of his rifle forward and squeezed off a shot at Wagner's tree. He quickly worked the lever and seated another bullet.

Schneck fired two more shots that sizzled over Brad's head with a whirring sound. He heard the bullets plow into the ground far behind him.

"Let's get the hell out of here, Otto," Wagner gruffed. "I'm plumb empty."

"Me, too," Schneck said.

A second later, both men darted from behind their trees and dashed to their horses a few yards away.

"Where to?" Wagner said as he climbed into the saddle and ducked low over the horn.

"LaPorte," Schneck snapped back. "We can buy ammunition there."

Schneck hauled himself into his saddle, and the two men wheeled their horses and scrambled toward the road.

Brad shot once more at the fleeing men, but he didn't have a clear shot. Too many aspens between him and the two riders. His bullet smacked into a tree, and then the two men galloped down the road at full speed.

The hoofbeats got softer and softer until they faded like audience whispers when the first curtain opens. The silence welled up around Brad as he strained to hear anything else. He waited there for several moments to see if they might return. Finally, he stood up. He brushed the loose dirt from his buckskins, then walked around the tree to retrieve his hat. He picked it up and examined it. There was a small ragged hole near the edge of the brim. He put the hat back on his head and walked to the place where he had tied up Ginger. The horse pawed the ground with its right front hoof and nickered softly. Brad stuck the rifle in its boot and led the horse back down to the rocks. He stretched to reach the shotgun, grabbed its looped strap, and slung it over his saddle horn. He walked down to the flat, climbed into the saddle, then turned the horse down the road in pursuit of Schneck and Wagner.

He knew where they were going, and he knew it would be a long ride. He did not rule out the possibility that the two men might be waiting in ambush for him somewhere along the way. They might have been out of rifle cartridges, but they still had their pistols and he had seen cartridges on their gun belts.

So Brad rode with caution, his senses alert, in the glowing

sunlight. The clouds were still drifting off to the east, and he expected there would be rain that evening.

He rode into the tiny settlement of LaPorte at the confluence of the Poudre and the South Platte just at dusk. The brilliant sunset was a flaming glow off to the west, streaming golden rays into a blue sky devoid of clouds. The darkness came swiftly, and the mercantile store was just closing. The merchant was locking the door when Brad rode up to the hitch rail.

The man turned the key in the lock and turned to face Brad. He stuck the key in his pocket and shifted the satchel he carried in one hand to the other.

"Did you see two men ride through here?" Brad asked. "I think they wanted to buy rifle ammunition."

"Yep," the man said. "Them two came into the store wantin' to buy Winchester ca'tridges. I told them I was plumb out. Ain't huntin' season, and I ain't reordered what I sold last fall. They was both plumb put out about it."

"Did they say where they were headed?"

"Nope, not exactly." The man walked down the steps and stood looking up at Brad. "But they wanted to know where they could buy some of them ca'tridges and I told them they might have to go to Fort Collins or Denver."

"Why Denver?" Brad asked.

"'Cause they ain't but one or two stores in Fort Collins that might have a box or two of Winchester ca'tridges and they'd likely be closed by the time they got there."

"Where in Denver?" Brad asked.

"You sure are nosy, mister," the man said. "But I told them they might go to Larimer Street. You can buy pretty much anything on Larimer at any time of day or night."

"Thanks," Brad said and turned Ginger away from the rail as if to ride out.

"Somethin' else you might want to know, feller," the man said. "Seein' how nosy you be."

"Those two men are criminals and I'm a private detective."

"Well, then, that explains it," the man said.

"So, what else can you tell me?"

"Whilst them two was in the store, another feller come in all covered with dust and sweatin' like a plow horse, just a-jabberin' away like a dadgummed magpie."

"Who was he? What was he gabbing about?" Brad asked.

"Well, sir, I think he was trail boss of a herd of cattle. And one of them what come in might have been the owner of them cattle 'cause the trail boss feller said the herd he was drivin' down from Cheyenne had stampeded a few miles north of here and run right on past LaPorte. He said they just kept a-runnin' and they were tryin' to get 'em all herded up again."

"Did he say where the herd was?"

"Yep, sure did. He had rode on back where they had most of 'em bunched up. I know the place. It's real spooky, you ask me."

"What's the place?"

"West of Denver they's a jumble of great big old rocks that are as red as that sunset yonder. The cattle run in there and they're havin' one hell of a time getting 'em out."

"So, what did the man you think was the owner say?"

"I think his name was Shank, or somethin' like that. He called the other man with him 'Jim' and he says to Jim that they better get on down there to them red rocks and help get that herd collected and drive them up to Poudre Canyon."

"So, then, the three of them rode out after that, I reckon," Brad said.

"Sure did. I sold them some bear claws and some elk jerky, and they moseyed on acrost the bridge and headed down toward Denver."

"Thanks, mister," Brad said. "You've been a big help."

"I ought to charge hard coin for such good information," the man said, "but this evenin' it's on the house."

Brad touched a finger to the brim of his hat and turned Ginger.

"Lots of luck, stranger," the man called after Brad. "I hope you got you a slicker 'cause it's goin' to rain like a cow pissin' on a flat rock down Denver way."

Brad raised a hand and waved without looking back.

To the south and east, after he crossed the wooden bridge over the South Platte, he saw the lumbering leviathans of dark black thunder clouds. Below them, hanging like shrouds, were streaks of black that indicated it was already raining. And he would ride into it in a couple of hours. There was no wind, and the storm was stalled. He could not yet hear the thunder, but he saw silver streaks of lightning forking jagged latticework in the swollen hearts of the storm clouds.

He could barely read the tracks on the road, but just before dark, he noted the tracks of three horses heading south, and there was no wind to blow them away. He stopped after an hour, when he began to hear the rumble of thunder. He broke out his slicker and slipped it on, remounted, and patted Ginger softly on the neck.

"You'll wish you had blinders on before this is over," he said to the horse. Ginger bobbed his head and responded to the gentle poke of Brad's spur in his left flank.

The road stretched out before Brad, empty, and disappeared in the darkness that crawled across the land like a giant shadow, engulfing the land in a sea of blackness.

THIRTY

❧

Chester Loomis sagged in the saddle, red-eyed from lack of sleep, five days of beard stubble on his suntanned chin, his clothing soggy from sweat. Beside him rode Jim Wagner and Otto Schneck. They all wore yellow slickers as they headed toward the massive thunderstorm that was hurling down rain along the foothills, jabbing huge lances of lightning into the ground.

"The herd is strung out for a good twenty miles or so, Otto," Chet said, his voice wavering up and down from the jogging of his equally weary horse, a saddle-sore sorrel cutting horse with clipped mane and tail. "We ought to be seein' some of 'em any minute now."

"It's a good thing you got across the Platte first before the cows stampeded," Wagner said.

"That's about the only thing Chet did right," Schneck snarled. "How in hell did you manage to stampede three thousand head of cattle?"

"Them cows was spooked the whole way down here,"

Loomis said. "Like they was just waitin' for that first crack of thunder."

"You mean that's what got 'em to runnin'?" Wagner said.

"Yeah, some of them black clouds broke away, and it was like watchin' a big old monster rise up outen the mountains and come snarlin' down on top of us," Loomis said. "Hell, it moved fast as the D and RG packin' freight cars on a downhill run. And then, there was that damned twister."

"Twister?" Schneck rasped.

"Twister or big old dust devil, I don't know what," Loomis said. "Whilst we was a-tryin' to turn the herd up front what had stampeded, a twister come a-boilin' up out of nowhere and played hob with the main body of the herd and there was cows bawlin' and runnin' like hell."

"And, you couldn't stop 'em?" Wagner said, in disbelief.

"Like a damned river, they was," Loomis said. "Thousands of cows a-bawlin', scared half to death, just runnin' like the devil was a-chasin' 'em. They knocked down two of my outriders what was flankin' 'em and just kept on a-runnin' like their tails was on fire."

"What did you do to try and stop the herd?" Schneck asked, his anger mounting to the boiling point.

"Hell, we tried stampedin' 'em back on theirselves. Shot our rifles at 'em, even killed one or two of the leaders. Nothin' could stop 'em or turn 'em. It was like every head had gone completely loco, crazy as whorehouse bedbugs."

"Where in hell is the better part of my herd?" Schneck asked, his neck bulging like a bullfrog's.

"We got 'em stopped, finally, in them red rocks west of Denver about fifteen miles. But we got cattle scattered all through these damned foothills. I got men tryin' to round 'em up when they find a bunch. But hell, Otto, I'm shorthanded. It's goin' to take a week to find 'em all. Only we ain't goin' to."

For a long time none of the men said anything. They rode along the foothills while lightning flashed in the black thunderheads, lighting up the hills and the flat like a photographer's phosphorus powder. They began to see the silhouettes of men on horseback driving small clumps of cattle, chasing strays and yelling at the tops of their lungs. The cattle they saw were still scared and hard to handle. The three men kept riding until they came to a larger group of cattle and two men trying to bed them down in a shallow ravine between two low hills.

"Ho, Jerry," Loomis called to one of the men. "What you got?"

Jerry Finnerty rode up to Loomis and pulled a ready-made out of his pocket and struck a match.

"We got a hunnert head we're tryin' to box up and hold until Cal Jennings can get the main herd out of that red rock nightmare and head 'em back this way."

"Any cattle still loose between here and the red rocks?" Loomis asked.

Finnerty shrugged and puffed on his cigarette. "Damned if I know," he said. "We turned nigh a thousand head back into them red rocks and they was swallered up. We ain't got enough men to box 'em all in, even down there. Whitsett's got a bad leg. Smashed it against one of them big old rocks when a bunch of cows run at him."

"You go on back there and get them cows bedded down, Jerry," Loomis said. "We'll go on to the red rocks and see if we can't give Whitsett a hand."

"That storm has already hit 'em all in there," Finnerty said and tossed his burning cigarette to the ground. He looked even more haggard than Loomis, and it was plain to see that his temper bore a short fuse. "It's goin' to take a dozen men a week to find all them cows. Them red rocks are big and run ever' which away like they was tossed there deliberate."

"Maybe we better help you, Jerry, while we're here," Wagner said.

"We could use another hand or two, that's for damn sure," Finnerty said.

"Boss?" Wagner said.

"You stay here and help Finnerty, and who else is here?" Schneck said.

"Dub Neiman," Finnerty said. "He's plumb tuckered, like me, but he's a game old cowhand."

Schneck snorted. Dub was at least sixty years old, crippled by rheumatism, and looked a hundred. He had kept him on because he was an old hand and knew cattle like he knew the wrinkles in his withered skin.

"Yeah, Jim," Schneck said, finally. "You'd better help Dub and Jerry. Chet and I will ride on to those red rocks. I have to see them for myself, find out just what in hell we're up against."

"All right, Otto," Wagner said. "Jerry, let's see what we can do with these cows you got here."

The two men rode off in the darkness and met up with Dub, who was zigzagging his cutting horse back and forth in front of several cows who stood there like frozen statues ready to bolt past him at the first opportunity.

Schneck and Loomis rode on past them and into the first curtain of rain.

Lightning bolts crashed all around them, and their horses jumped at every flash. They bent their heads down, unaware that less than a quarter mile to their rear, a lone rider was on their trail.

Brad tucked his binoculars back inside his slicker. He had watched as Wagner left with another man, leaving Schneck and his trail boss to ride on. He saw, in the dim light, the shreds of black clouds dripping down as the thunderheads loosed their water. Soon, he thought, the rain would hit the place where Wagner was going and another man was trying to hold dozens of cattle in check or drive them into that ravine.

Three against one, he thought, as he turned to ride close to the lone man on the cutting horse holding a dozen head in check as Wagner and the other rider rode to join him.

"I'll never get a better chance," he said to himself.

He knew where Schneck was headed with his trail boss.

But Wagner had to pay for his part in the slaughter of the Basque women and children and the two men.

He closed the distance between him and Wagner.

He looked to where he had last seen Schneck and the trail boss. When the lightning struck again, the two were gone, vanished into the night and the rain. Thunder boomed, and the rain lashed down at him, pattering softly at first and then flooding from the sky in long, thick streams as if a trapdoor had opened in the belly of the clouds and released a deluge that would have scared the hell out of Noah himself.

Brad turned his horse and headed in the direction where Wagner and the other man had gone.

He loosened the thong around his neck but did not pull out his rattles. With the noise of the thunder he would probably not need them. But he touched the butt of his pistol and loosened it slightly in its holster.

He would give Wagner a chance to surrender, even though he had shown no mercy toward the Basques. If he did not throw down his pistol, then Brad would call him out.

It was not vengeance he sought, he told himself, but justice.

Justice for all those souls lying back there dead in Poudre Canyon.

Lightning flashed again, close. Brad saw the cows finally turn and dash into the ravine to join the others of their kind.

Wagner's form stood out like a man caught by light and, etched on Brad's retinas in some bizarre tintype, his face turned toward Brad for that one instant when hunter and prey sight each other for the first and last time.

THIRTY-ONE

~

Jim Wagner squinched his eyes against the rain. He saw the approaching rider but could not identify him. The man's yellow slicker stood out like a beacon in the rain.

"Who's that?" he said to Finnerty.

Finnerty turned his head and saw the rider through a glaze of rain. He shook his head.

"Damned if I know," he said. "He's too far away. Maybe one of the boys comin' to help."

"Maybe," Wagner said.

"I got to go help Dub, Jim. You find out who it is, and we'll put him to work right quick."

Wagner waited as Finnerty rode off to help Dub drive the balking cattle into the ravine.

Brad rode up to within fifteen feet of Wagner. He stopped his horse and Wagner urged his own horse closer by a few feet.

"You one of Loomis's hands?" Wagner asked.

"I just hired on," Brad said.

"Well, come on, then. We got work to do," Wagner replied.

"You bet we have work to do, Wagner." Brad spread the flap of his slicker to one side so that he could draw his pistol. "You and I have some business to attend to."

"Huh?"

"You heard me. Some unfinished business."

"You ain't makin' no sense, pard."

"Well, there are the dead horses," Brad said. "And the women, two dead men, and several children."

"What in the hell are you talkin' about, man?" Wagner exploded.

"I'm here to arrest you for murder, Wagner. I'm a private detective. I'm duly sworn as an officer of the court."

"You go straight to hell, mister," Wagner spat.

"Surrender right now, or I'll have to figure you're a fugitive fleeing from the law."

"I'll show you who's a damned fugitive," Wagner said and flipped his slicker open to draw his sidearm.

Brad pulled his pistol from his holster and cocked it on the rise. He leveled it at Wagner's chest, plumb center, and squeezed the trigger. The Colt belched flame and spewed lead and sparks within ten feet of Wagner. The barrel of the foreman's pistol was still half sheathed in the holster when the bullet struck him just left of his heart.

He jerked to his right with the force of the bullet and gasped a dying breath. The bullet ripped through ribs, nicked a corner of his heart, and exploded the veins and arteries connected to that organ. Blood spurted from the wound and splattered his slicker with dozens of red splashes as if the raincoat had erupted with a skin rash.

Wagner's hand went limp, his fingers splayed away from the butt of his pistol, and the .45 slid back into its holster.

Wagner pitched sideways out of his saddle, and he fell to the ground. Rain beat a muffled tattoo on his slicker as a thin plume of smoke spiraled upward out of the barrel of Brad's gun.

"Payback," Brad murmured.

Dub and Finnerty rode up. They both looked down at the body of Wagner.

Then Finnerty reached for the rifle in his boot.

"I'd think long and hard before you pull that rifle out," Brad said. "Wagner and Schneck murdered a whole bunch of women and children, plus a couple of sheepherders, up in Poudre Canyon. I gave Wagner a chance to surrender and he went for his gun. I shot him."

"You a lawman?" Finnerty asked.

"Detective," Brad said.

Finnerty's hand rested on the butt of his rifle, but he made no move to jerk it from its boot.

"This ain't none of our business," Dub said. "Let's get back to them cows."

"Good advice," Brad said. "Or else you can join Wagner there on the ground."

"Mister, I don't know who in hell you are, but you don't sound like no star packer to me." Finnerty grabbed the butt of his rifle. Dub reached over and grabbed his partner's wrist.

"Don't chance it," Dub said to Finnerty.

"I'll give you three seconds to turn your horses around and ride back to that ravine," Brad said. "Otherwise, I empty two saddles." He cocked his pistol and they all heard the click as the hammer locked into place.

"We're goin', mister," Dub said. He turned his own horse and grabbed the bridle on Finnerty's horse and turned the horse's head.

The two men rode off through the rain and disappeared from sight.

Brad ejected the empty hull and replaced it with a fresh cartridge. He set the hammer down between two cylinders of the magazine and holstered his pistol.

He rode off, heading south, as the rainfall got heavier and gusts of wind began to lash at him. He closed up his slicker and pulled his hat on tighter.

"One down," he said to his horse, "and one to go."

Ginger whickered softly, dipping his head as a foil against the wind.

Sheets of rain staggered across the trail and washed away all the tracks.

But Brad knew that the night was as black and wet for Schneck as it was for him. He would not seek shelter but ride through it until he caught up with Schneck and his trail boss. If they stopped to get out of the storm, that would make Brad's journey shorter. If not, he would catch up to them eventually.

He was certain of that. All Schneck was thinking about was his cattle.

And when Schneck found them, Brad would find Schneck.

That's when he would kill a snake if the man didn't surrender.

Brad had a strong hunch that Schneck would not give himself up.

And he didn't give a damn.

As far as he was concerned, Schneck didn't even deserve a choice of whether to surrender or die.

Payback was payback.

And Schneck owed a big debt.

THIRTY-TWO

∾

Vivelda and Thor rode into the lower valley late in the afternoon. The clouds had all drifted out of the mountains and were hovering over the foothills, their fluffy folds turning blacker by the minute, as if the sky itself was becoming enraged.

Mike and Joe saw the two and walked away from the chuck wagon with coffee cups in their hands.

Joe reached up and helped Vivelda alight from the horse she was riding.

"I have bad news," Sorenson said. "Vivelda here is the only one who escaped alive."

He dismounted and stood there before the two dumbstruck, bewildered men.

Vivelda began to sob. Joe put his arm around her but could not speak.

"All dead?" Mike said.

Sorenson nodded. "Every last one. Horses, men, women, and all the little kids."

"Oh no," Mike said, in disbelief.

"It—it's true," Vivelda said. "It was awful. I—I ran away. Brad and Thor found me."

"I want to hear the whole story," Mike said. "Did you see what happened, Sorenson?"

"No. Brad and I got there too late to save anyone. We tracked Vivelda here and found her hiding in some rocks."

"Where's Brad?" Joe asked.

"He's tracking Schneck and his foreman, Jim Wagner. We got two of the men who shot and killed all those people."

Joe crossed himself.

"Tell me what happened, Vivelda," Mike said. "Do you want some tea or coffee? Something to eat? You're all cut up."

She shook her head. Her legs were weak, and she started to collapse, but Joe grabbed her and held her up.

Vivelda told them all that she had seen and heard from the beginning of the attack until she ran away and was found by Sorenson and Storm. She sobbed throughout the entire account, and both of the Basque men were touched by her painful recollection.

"You're going to need four horses to take down there to pull those two wagons back up here," Sorenson said. "I'll help you gather up the dead and load them into the wagons. It's not a pretty sight."

"Most of the men are in the upper valley with the sheep. Joe and I will get the horses and go with you. Vivelda, will you be all right? Renata and Nestor can look after you."

"I—I'll be all right," she stammered.

Joe led her over to the chuck wagon where a curious Renata was standing with her husband, Nestor, wondering why Vivelda had come back with that tall blue-eyed man with the funny accent.

Joe explained what had happened, and Renata made the sign of the cross with her shaking hand while Nestor's eyes filled up with tears. Renata enfolded Vivelda in her arms and hugged her while they both wept.

Joe walked back and followed Mike and Thor as they headed to the stables leading the two horses.

"We can use this one on one of the wagons," Mike said.

"We might have to use a mule," Joe said. "I got a horse and Mikel has a horse, but . . ."

"We have enough," Mike said, cutting his friend's dialogue short.

Within a half hour, the three men were ready to make the journey down Poudre Canyon. Joe rode over and said goodbye to Nestor, who told them that Renata had taken Vivelda into the cabin where she had last stayed.

"It'll be dark before we get back, Nestor," Joe said. "You take good care of Vivelda."

"We will," Nestor said, his eyes still brimming with tears.

It was turning cold, and the canyon was filling with shadows by the time the three men came to the place of the slaughter. Joe and Mike were horrified at what they saw, women and children scattered, stiff and dead, around the wagons, the horses beginning to reek, the two dead men looking like wooden mannequins. Buzzards flapping up into the remaining radiant shafts of sunlight on broad black wings, coyotes skulking off into the timber. It was hard for the men to look at those bodies that had already been violated by the scavengers.

Joe and Thor struggled with the traces on the dead horses and swung the wagon tongues back straight. They hooked up the horses and one mule to the two wagons, then helped load the dead into the passenger wagon. They did this with solemn reverence, their faces grim and stolid as fire-blackened iron.

When Joe and Mike lifted the stiff corpse of Leda and carried her to the wagon, both men wept uncontrollably and without shame.

"Such a tragedy," Joe sobbed.

Mike could not speak. His throat was constricted as if he had swallowed a gallon of astringent. He could not look at Leda's pale and bloodless face, the wound in her body, the dried blood, the soiled dress.

He thought of happier times when she and her husband were part of his family. He thought of the night before he had sent all the women and children down the mountain where he thought they would be safe. He cursed himself for that misguided deed. And his hatred of the cattlemen, especially Otto Schneck, rose black and monstrous in his mind.

Yet he knew that such blinding hatred was dangerous. Such a rage could lead to further bloodshed that would solve nothing.

He thought of what his father had told him once when he was a young boy living in the Pyrenees, a shepherd boy with his own little flock to tend.

Enos Garaboxosa was then a very old man, in his sixties, and Mikel was about thirteen.

"Guard what you think, Mikel," he said after his son had been fighting with another shepherd boy. "If you hate, you give off hate and hate comes back to you. If you give off love, then love comes back to you and wipes out the hate."

"But that boy hit me," Mikel had wailed.

"And you hit him back. So, his hit made you hit. His anger gave you anger and you gave him back his anger. You must break such chains or you will live a sad and lonely life."

"I do not see how," Mikel had said to his father.

"That is the way of the universe, my son. There is an energy in the heavens, a force that comes in sunlight and in rain. It is a force that we cannot see, but it guides our lives here on earth. The Father of All made it so. We, like the trees and the ocean and the rivers, the grass, the sheep, are all influenced by the stars and planets high up in the sky. The moon raises the rivers and the ocean tides, and it raises our blood as well."

"I do not understand such things, Pap," Mikel had said.

"Ah, nor do many, but if you believe in that hidden force which is in all things, you will live a long and happy life. It is this force which makes a seed grow into grass or into a flower. It is this force which tells the bee to make honey and the mothers to make milk for their babies. It is a powerful force, and it is invisible. You cannot see this force, but it is everywhere, and it is in all things."

Mike wanted to kill all the cattlemen, but in that instant he heard again his father's words. They came to him over the years and he knew, in the deepest part of him, that his father had much wisdom and that he was right. It did him no good to hate. That is what killed all these people. Hate.

Only now, hate had a different name.

That name was Schneck.

The Snake.

He and Joe laid the body of Leda in the wagon, and each said a silent prayer for her eternal soul. Thor carried the body of a small boy up to the wagon and laid him next to Leda.

It went on that way as the sun fled the sky and streamed its rays into the aching blueness, showered a shimmering golden glow behind the snow-clad peaks and left the shadows to grow and thicken in the canyon, to darken the Poudre to a crystal mélange of subdued colors except for the foaming whitecaps that seemed impervious to darkness or shadow. They flocked the tumbling waters like small mantles of white lace.

When the wagons were loaded, the men turned them and headed back up the canyon. Joe drove the supply wagon while Mike took the wagon of the dead, with their horses tethered behind each. Thor rode ahead. He felt as if he were in a funeral procession. The buzzards had disappeared from the sky, and along the river, there was a feeling of solitude and emptiness. He did not know any of the dead, but he saw the effect they had on the two men, and he could feel their grief, the deep sadness in their hearts.

It was full dark when they reached camp, and he helped Joe and Mike lay a tarp over the wagon with the dead and tie it down.

"We will take turns standing guard over our people," Mike said.

"I will take the first watch," Joe said.

"I will take a watch if you'll let me," Sorenson said. "I feel some obligation."

"You need not," Mike said. "But you can relieve me in the morning. You have had a longer day than I."

"That is true," Joe said. "You eat, Thor, and you get some sleep, eh?"

"I could use some shut-eye, I reckon," Sorenson said.

They ate a solemn supper that Renata prepared for them, and Vivelda sat with them and picked at her food. She kept glancing over at the tarp-encased wagon with a disconsolate look on her face.

"I wonder where Brad is now," she said as they all listened to the thunderclaps in the distance, the rollicking rumble of a storm over the foothills and down on the plain. "I wonder if he has caught up with the Snake."

"I wonder, too," Sorenson said. "But I know he won't quit until he's caught both Schneck and Wagner. He don't have no quit in him, that man."

They were silent after that, and when Sorenson put down his bedroll in one of the empty cabins, he fell asleep with the sound of thunder rolling across the sky like empty barrels in an attic.

The last thing he heard was the far-off bleating of a sheep, and it gave him a strange feeling of utter peace just before he dropped off into the bottomless abyss of sleep.

THIRTY-THREE

❧

Schneck and Loomis rode into a light rainsquall that soon turned into a frog strangler. Then they felt the sting of the rain on their faces as the wind rose up like some avenging banshee and battered them with howling torrents that drenched their slickers and turned their hats into sodden rain gutters.

"Looks like we done rode into a full-bore, .60-caliber howler," Loomis said.

"Yeah, so what?"

"So, we're goin' to have a lot of wet cattle in the mornin'."

"They'll dry out," Schneck said.

"You still got that detective in your craw, Otto?"

"What if I do?"

"It don't make your disposition any better."

"My disposition is none of your business," Schneck said.

"Well, it could use a little sugar on it. You want to hole up and wait out this storm under a rock or somethin'?"

"No, damn it. We'll ride on, Loomis. It'll be just as cold and wet under a rock ledge."

"Look, Otto, I'm real sorry about that stampedin', but I did all I could, and it wasn't my fault."

"I am not angry at you, Chet. Hell, I've had cattle stampede on me a couple of times."

"Then what're you mad at, Otto? That jasper on your tail?"

"Yeah, him and those damn sheepherders. If I hadn't run out of rifle cartridges, that Sidewinder would be wolf meat."

"I ain't packin' a Winchester, and my rifle's .40 caliber."

"I know."

"Maybe some of the hands can help you out when we meet up with them."

"That might be too late. I can feel that bastard breathing down my neck. I'd like to wring his neck."

Schneck thought back to his boyhood in Andernach, Germany, and the summers he spent on his uncle Gustav's farm. He loved to wring the necks of the chickens when they wanted some for Sunday supper. He also liked to use a hammer and kill the rabbits when his aunt Helga made rabbit stew or hasenpfeffer. Later, he trapped small birds in wooden boxes held up on a stick with a string attached to it. He put seeds under the box and, when a bird hopped in to get at the seeds, he pulled the string and caught the bird. He would hold a bird in his hand and squeeze its breast until it gasped for breath and died. Killing small animals gave him much pleasure, but he liked to make them suffer first. He would have liked to have done that with those Basque women and children, but he wanted to send a strong message to Garaboxosa. He hoped the bastard had gotten the message and would remember him when he buried all those dead people.

Maybe, he thought, all those sheep would be out of the mountains by the time he drove his cattle herd up there in a day or two.

"Well," Loomis said as he wiped water from his mouth, "maybe this Sidewinder is holed up somewhere hisself, or has just give up."

"I have a feeling he's not a man to give up, Chet."

"Then, get a bead on him when he shows up and blow out his candle."

"I had the bastard. I had him dead to rights, and I ran out of bullets. So did Jim."

"Too bad. But you can't cry over spilt milk, Otto. What's done is done and you can't change it."

"No, but I'd like to have another chance at Sidewinder."

"Maybe you'll get another chance by and by," Loomis said.

"I hope I do," Schneck said and meant it.

The rain whipped at them. The wind snarled and railed at them with increasing ferocity. The horses splashed in large puddles, and their hooves slipped off wet rocks and they staggered and stumbled, drooping their heads as if they were pulling plows.

Loomis thought that it was not a fit night for man or beast.

But both man and beast were in it, and he kept hoping Otto would relent and let him seek shelter for both of them.

He knew damned well that the German was a hardhead and wouldn't stop to rest or dry out, no matter what.

It was going to be a long night.

THIRTY-FOUR

∽

Sorenson awoke to the sound of a shotgun blast, a high-pitched yelp, and angry men's voices.

He sat up in his bedroll and groped for his boots in the dark. He slipped his feet into them, picked up his gun belt next to his pillow, stood up, and strapped on his pistol. He strode outside and walked to the wagon where the dead lay under the tarp that glistened with dew. He smelled the acrid aroma of exploded gunpowder, and there was a ghostly wisp of smoke hanging in the air a few feet from the wagon.

Moonlight glazed the back of a man who was bent over something on the ground a dozen yards away. The man stood up and looked toward Sorenson.

"Wolf," Joe said.

Sorenson walked over and saw the dead timber wolf lying stretched out. Joe held a sawed-off shotgun in his left hand that reeked of burned cordite.

"It must be a good eight or nine feet long," Sorenson said.

Joe had stretched the tail full length and placed the head in a straight line with its body.

"Big one," Joe said.

"Just one?" Sorenson asked. He grazed his fingers over his beard stubble, which felt like sandpaper.

"Just this one. Sneaked up on me. I was sitting under the wagon when I saw him."

Sorenson looked up at the starry sky, the shining half-moon, the sparkling band of the Milky Way. Venus shone like a brilliant diamond, and he could see the faint orange glow of Mars winking in the black void beyond the moon.

"Time for me to relieve you, Joe," Sorenson said. "Get some sleep."

"Do you want the shotgun? In case you see another wolf?"

"No. My six-gun will be enough."

"I will sleep, then. I am glad this one did not go for the sheep."

"Good night, Joe," Sorenson said.

"Good night, Thor."

Joe walked away toward one of the log cabins. He opened the door and disappeared inside. Sorenson walked back to the wagon and leaned against the bed. The tarp made a crackling sound when he put his weight against it. He could smell the decomposing bodies underneath the fabric. The wagon reeked of a faint, cloying, somewhat sweet smell that was sickening to him. He tried not to think of the stiff bodies stacked in the wagon bed like cordwood.

Two hours later, the sky began to pale in the east. Light washed out the stars as it crept across the arc of the sky, and the moon became a pale shell, as faded as a late summer flower, its skeletal shape suspended in a sea of cerulean blue. Mike walked from his cabin to the wagon where Sorenson stood, gazing at the shadows crawling downward from the high country, revealing brilliant white peaks that seemed to glow from some inner fluorescence.

"Good morning, Thor," Mike said. "How'd you like to take a ride with me?"

Sorenson turned and gave Mike his full attention.

"Maybe. Where you going?"

"To the upper valley where we drove most of the sheep yesterday. I need some diggers to help bury our dead. And some of the shepherds there have wives and children among the dead."

Sorenson thought about it for a moment.

"Yes, Mike, I'll ride up there with you, but then I'm going on to the other valley where Schneck is grazing his cattle."

"Are you going back there to work for Schneck?"

"Not on your life, Mike. There's someone I want to see up there."

Mike rubbed his chin as he thought about what Sorenson had told him.

"The Mexican?" Mike said.

"Yes. Jorge Verdugo. The man who came down here under false pretenses and worked for you, suppered with you, and then betrayed you."

"You know that to be true?"

"Yes. Schneck sent him down here to spy on you. I think Schneck planned to come down here and murder the women and children, but after Verdugo told him they were all leaving, he changed his plans."

"What will you do with the Mexican?"

"I'm going to bring him down here to help dig graves. And I want him to see the people he caused to die. The people who befriended him."

"Some of my men may not take kindly to your bringing the Mexican down here at such a solemn and holy time."

"Verdugo needs to know what his words to Schneck caused to happen."

"Just tell him," Mike said.

Sorenson snorted in derision.

"Verdugo is not a very smart man. My telling him might just wash over him and seep away like water down a hole."

"I see," Mike said. "Bring him down then, but I won't be responsible for what happens if the men find out what he did."

"I won't tell them if you won't, Mike."

"I will not tell them. But I may put a rope around his neck and hang him from one of those big junipers."

"If you do, I'll help you string him up," Sorenson said.

Less than an hour later, with sourdough biscuits, coffee, and mutton in their bellies, Mike and Thor rode across the valley and up the trail to the higher ground. The sun was high and drenched the grasses and the trees with warmth and golden sunshine, burning off the dew and making the green hues as radiant as emeralds.

"Tell me about Minnesota," Mike said when they were riding through the timber that gave them shade among the shimmering shafts of sunlight. "I have never been there. What is it like?"

"It is a land of many lakes, although I guess some of them are no more than ponds. The lakes are teeming with fish. There are no mountains, like here. Just a lot of lakes and a legend about them."

"What is this legend?"

"They say a giant created the land and lived there. They call him Paul Bunyan. They say that the lakes were made by his heavy footprints when he walked the land. They explain everything unusual there was caused by Paul Bunyan."

Mike laughed, and Sorenson joined him.

"Perhaps it is so," Mike said.

"Minnesota has many Swedes and Norwegians and Germans living there, and I think the early settlers brought their fairy tales with them across the ocean. Many of them believe in little folks and ancient gods and strange creatures."

"And giants," Mike said with a smile.

"Just that one giant, Mike."

Sorenson left Mike in the upper valley and rode on to the cattle camp. He found Verdugo working in the stable and called him out.

"What is it you want, Sorenson?" Verdugo asked.

"Saddle up a horse and ride with me, Jorge," Sorenson said. It was not a request, but a command.

"Why? Where do we go?"

"I'm going to show you something, and I have some work for you."

"Does Snake send you?"

"No, Schneck didn't send me. You get crackin', Jorge, or I'll take a quirt to your worthless Mexican hide."

Verdugo seemed to recall the beating he took at the hands of the Swede and nodded.

"I will go with you," he said.

A half hour later the two were riding at a good clip through the timber. They descended into the lower valley to see men digging graves, wielding their shovels against buried rocks and hard, grassy dirt.

"What is this?" Verdugo asked.

"Get off your horse and I'll find you a shovel, Jorge," Sorenson said.

"What are they digging?" Verdugo asked.

"You'll see."

Sorenson led Verdugo over to where Mike was standing. The wagon had been pulled up close to the graveyard. The tarp was still on it, and it stood in the shade of the pines.

"Do you have a shovel for this man, Mike?" Sorenson asked. "He wants to do some digging."

"There's an extra shovel on the ground next to that spruce tree," Mike said.

"Do you pay me for this?" Verdugo asked.

"You'll get something out of it, Jorge," Sorenson said as he walked him to where the shovel lay.

Joe put Verdugo to work. He told him where to dig and

how deep. Verdugo sniffed the air as he drove the shovel into the ground and turned the soil.

"What is that I smell?" he asked Sorenson.

"That's what you're burying after you dig that hole, Jorge," Sorenson said.

"I do not understand."

Mike stood close by and nodded to Sorenson.

"You want to see, Jorge?" Sorenson said. "Come with me, then."

Sorenson walked Jorge to the wagon and untied a couple of tie-down ropes. He shoved Jorge up to the tailgate and let him look at what was in the wagon.

Verdugo recoiled at the sight of the dead people lying on the bed, stiff as heavy lumber, their faces drained of blood, their eyes fixed and dull as dirty marbles. He recoiled as if he had been bitten by some unseen animal.

"That is what you did, Jorge. When you told Schneck about these people going down the canyon. Schneck, Wagner, and two others murdered these people, and now they are going to be buried. You are digging one of the graves."

"Jesus, I did not know," Verdugo said.

"You knew, Jorge. You told Schneck, and you knew what he meant to do."

Verdugo buried his face in his hands.

"I am so sorry," he said. "So sorry."

"Get back to digging, Jorge," Sorenson said and shoved him back toward the graveyard.

Verdugo stumbled for a few feet and then walked to where he had been digging and picked up the shovel.

Mike came over to talk to Sorenson.

"What are you going to do with Verdugo when we are all finished here and we have said good-bye to our friends?" Mike asked.

"I'm going to tie him up and wait for Brad to return. We'll take Verdugo down to Denver, and we'll watch him hang. He's just as much a criminal as Schneck."

"We could hang him here," Mike said.

"It would be quicker, but if he hangs in Denver, some of those cowhands will see him die and maybe they'll think twice before they try to run your sheep out of the mountains."

"I think you are a wise man, Thor. Let this Mexican be an example to many who would drive us away."

Sorenson nodded and dug a plug of tobacco from his shirt pocket. He cut off a chunk and stuck it in his mouth.

Mike walked away and spelled one of the diggers.

He said prayers over the dead at high noon. Verdugo sobbed as the shepherds lowered the bodies, which were wrapped in linen sheets, into the ground. Some of the men dangled their beads and wept with their hats off.

Sheep bleated in the valley, and a swarm of buzzards wheeled in the sky as if they were pinned to an invisible merry-go-round, the tips of their wings like feathered fingers touching the cobalt sky.

Small birds chirped as they hopped on the grass, and a chipmunk whistled from the talus slope, sounding as forlorn as a lost waif calling its pet dog.

THIRTY-FIVE

∽

There was a trail leading to the strange conglomeration of iron-rich rocks where most of the stampeded cattle herd had wandered. Schneck and Loomis rode down the trail from the north. They began to see cattle in pairs, trios, and foursomes standing near small hills, their backs to the wind, their heads drooping, and their hides shedding rain.

The cattle seemed unmindful of the rolling thunder that pealed across the sky, or the occasional bolts of lightning that lanced the earth and the rocks.

When Schneck saw the huge red-hued rocks jutting at angles from the earth, he felt intimidated by their sheer size. There were cattle scattered all through the flat plain where the rocks were staggered like fallen monoliths. It was as if nature had dropped them all in a heap and then kicked them around like a child's blocks.

"Spooky place, ain't it?" Loomis said as they rode beneath a giant slab of rock that looked like the side of a large building. Rain splashed against its layered sides, and small

waterfalls cascaded from every crevice and small shelf. Water
ran everywhere in rippling rivulets, corkscrewing across
open land, leaving puddles at every turn and twist. The noise
of the rain on the gigantic rocks was loud enough, but the
wind howled over and under them while lightning danced in
the dark clouds like jagged lances hurled from some great
height. And the thunder was amplified by the rocks. Schneck
felt the concussive force of wind and thunder as Loomis lit
up with lightning flashes, then became a dark silhouette atop
a rain-slick horse.

They could hear cattle bawling in the recesses of the rocky
terrain and, finally, they saw a man on horseback, waving a
towel at several head, as if trying to drive them to some central
or prearranged location.

Loomis and Schneck rode up to the harried man, and he
turned and raised an empty hand.

"That you, Chet?" he said.

"Me and Mr. Schneck," Loomis shouted above the howl
of the wind and the boom of the thunder. "Where you drivin'
them cows, Rolly?"

"Hell, Chet, I ain't drivin' them nowhere. But Jess Crandall's got near a thousand head down in a jumble of rocks.
We're tryin' to get as much of the herd back together as we
can in this damned storm."

"We'll help you, Rolly," Loomis said. "I want to talk to
Jess anyway."

"It's hard to turn these cows with all the noise. Only reason they don't run like hell is that they're plumb tuckered
after twenty miles of runnin'."

"Do you have a rifle, Rolly?" Schneck asked. Rolly was
Earl Rollins, who worked on the Wyoming ranch and was a
pretty fair hand at roping and branding.

"No, sir. The less I pack on these drives, the less my old
horse has to work. You got that old single-shot .40, don't you,
Chet?"

"Yeah, but I only got three or four bullets for it. I carry it more or less for ballast."

Rolly laughed.

"Sorry, Mr. Schneck. I don't think any of the boys with me are packin' rifles. Just pistols."

"That means you're out of luck, Otto, if you're trying to roust up ca'tridges for that Winchester of your'n."

"I wanted to put a man on that trail to look for the Sidewinder," Schneck said.

"Sidewinder?" Rolly asked.

"Yeah, that's what they call him," Schneck said. "He's riding a strawberry roan and I expect him to come down that trail. I'm looking for someone to blow him out the saddle when he shows up."

"Hard to pick off a man with a pistol in this rain," Rolly said.

"Never mind, Rolly," Loomis said. "Let's drive these few head down to where Jess is. Anybody else down there?"

"I don't know, Boss. We got men and cattle scattered from hell to breakfast. But I think this is far as any of the cows got. Town of Morrison's right down the way, but none of 'em run that far."

The three men rounded up the few head and started to drive them to where Jess had a large part of the herd. Rolly rode drag, while Loomis and Schneck held in the flanks. The cattle lumbered off and joined the rest of the herd, filing into the main body with moos and throaty bellows.

"Where's Jess?" Schneck asked Loomis.

"Dunno. We'll look for him."

They found Crandall under an overhanging rock. He squatted on the ground while another man, Will Purdy, held up a slicker to block the wind. Jess and Will had gathered some firewood from the hills above the red rocks and some squaw wood from the pines higher up to use for kindling. Jess had three burned-out matches lying at the edge of the squaw wood and was striking a fourth match on the side of a matchbox.

The three men dismounted and stood around Jess to shield him from the lashing rain and the blowing wind.

"Need any help, Jess?" Loomis asked.

Crandall looked up and saw who had ridden up.

"Howdy, Chet, Mr. Schneck. I'm tryin' to light this fire so's we can warm our hands. Look at 'em."

He and Purdy held out their bone-white hands that were all wrinkled and puckered from the cold.

"Go right ahead, Jess," Loomis said.

Crandall struck another match, cupped the flaming tip in both hands, and set the fire in the dry squaw wood. They heard a crackling sound, and the tiny filaments on the branches caught fire. Jess leaned down and blew gently on the fire to spread it.

"Looks like you got it, Jess," Rolly said.

The larger branches caught fire and hissed as the rainwater evaporated into a fine mist. In a few minutes, they had a small campfire going. Purdy added more large limbs as it burned down. The men stood there for several minutes holding their wet, shriveled hands over the warmth. The smoke rose and flattened against the overhang and left a hazy smudge on its rosy surface.

"Who's tending the herd, Jess?" Schneck asked as he turned his flat hands over and raised them a bit higher away from the flickering flames.

"Ain't nobody here but me and Purdy," he said. "Them cattle ain't goin' nowhere tonight."

"They think they've found a home in these here rocks," Purdy said, half joking. "'Sides, they're worn out, same as us."

"Who's your best shot with a pistol, Jess?" Schneck asked.

The question caught Crandall by surprise. He looked at Rolly and Purdy, then at Loomis.

"Hell, I don't know, Mr. Schneck. We don't exactly hold

matches among us, what with chasin' cows all over creation and humpin' down the trail day and night."

"You don't need to be sarcastic, Jess," Schneck said. "I asked a question. I need an answer."

"Rolly?" Crandall asked, looking over at Rollins.

"I seen you shoot some airtights onc't or twice, Jess," Rolly said. "And Purdy there, he's a pretty good shot I reckon. Seen him tumble a coyote one night and a jackrabbit or two."

"Yeah," Crandall said. "Purdy, he's pretty good with a pistol, come to think of it."

"Hell, I ain't never shot nobody," Purdy said.

"Think you could dust a man off with that pistol of yours?" Schneck asked.

"If'n I was real close, I reckon I could," Purdy said.

"How's your eyesight, Will?" Schneck asked.

"Fair to middlin' I reckon. Say, you want me to kill this Sidewinder?"

"There's a fifty-dollar gold piece in it for you if you do, Will," Schneck said.

"Golly, Mr. Schneck, I'd kill my own granny for that kind of money. Only she's already dead and gone."

The men all laughed.

Schneck walked over and put an arm over Purdy's shoulder. He walked him a few feet away and put his mouth close to Purdy's ear.

"I want you to ride or walk back to the trail leading in here," he said. "Find a good big rock you can sit on and watch to see who comes down that trail. He's riding a strawberry roan. He's a tall fellow and is probably wearing a black or yellow slicker."

"Yes, sir," Purdy said.

"I want you to shoot him dead. Don't call out to him or ask him to stop. Just shoot him. Got that?"

"I got that. I'll do my damndest, Mr. Schneck."

"Get to it, then. When you get back with proof that Sidewinder is dead, I'll put a fifty-dollar gold piece in your hand."

"Golly, Mr. Schneck, that's right generous of you."

Purdy walked away to get his horse. Schneck returned to the campfire.

"Is he going to do it?" Loomis asked.

"I hope so. I saw a lot of big rocks by the side of that trail we rode in on. If Purdy's any kind of shot at all, he should take care of Mr. Sidewinder for us."

Loomis bit his tongue. He wanted to say, "You mean take care of him for *you*, Otto."

But he said nothing, and the men stood by the fire and waited out the storm as the huge rock loomed over them and poured silvery shawls of rain off its massive shoulder.

They watched the lightning streak over Denver and listened to the rumble of heavy thunder as the cattle milled and jostled each other under the drenching downpour that blackened their curly hides.

THIRTY-SIX

∽

For several miles, Brad thought he was either on a wild-goose chase or looking for the proverbial needle in the haystack. But the trackless mud began to show signs of hoofprints, small watery depressions in the trail made by four-footed animals packing weight. Soon, these turned into legible hoof marks that told him he was getting close.

The tracks were still blurred, but they were definable, even so. He rode on, ever more wary, his pulse racing. He saw a few head of cattle on the small hillsides, slipping and sliding to keep their footing on the soggy slopes.

Rocky outcroppings began to appear alongside the trail, which now showed a host of indecipherable gouges from the cloven hooves of cattle. The horse tracks were overlaid on these muddy hieroglyphics.

A jagged streak of lightning illuminated a man sitting atop one of the rocky cairns off to his left. He saw the back of a horse behind the rock. The man sitting there was wearing a gray slicker, and his hat was dripping rain from its brim.

Thunder rumbled from out on the plain, and Brad thought he could see the dim streetlamps of Denver in the misty distance.

The next time the lightning flashed, Brad saw that the man was standing up. And he had a pistol in his hand. He was looking uptrail in his direction.

Brad slid off his horse and slapped Ginger on the rump so that the horse would continue on its path.

Then he walked on the opposite side, matching the horse's gait. He knew the man on the rock could not see him since he had ducked down below his saddle.

When he drew close, Brad tugged on one rein. Ginger halted, its head twisted toward Brad.

Brad pulled out his rattles and shook them. He peered under his horse's neck and saw the man's head jerk toward the sound.

The man muttered something under his breath.

"You looking for somebody in particular?" Brad said.

"Huh? What's that?"

"Schneck send you?" Brad said.

The man swung his pistol toward Ginger.

Brad drew his Colt and hammered it back to full cock.

The man on the rock raised his arm to take aim at somebody he could not see.

"Big mistake, feller," Brad said. He lined up his sights and squeezed the trigger.

The pistol roared, and the man flew off the rock like a lizard blown off by a sudden gust of wind. His arms flailed and his pistol went flying. He hit the ground with a thud. Brad ran over to the other side of the rock and looked down at the stricken man.

Purdy's mouth moved, but no sound came out. Instead, there was a liquid gurgle in his throat. His eyes rolled back in their sockets as if he were trying to look inside himself. The gurgle turned into a faint rattle and his eyes turned glassy. A sound of air issued from his throat. He quivered all over and died.

Brad ejected the spent cartridge and replaced it with another full round.

"Is this all you've got, Schneck?" he said and mounted Ginger. He stuck his pistol back in its holster and pulled the shotgun, Snake Eyes, from its sheath. He cracked it open and saw the two shot shells seated in the firing chamber. He laid the sawed-off over his lap and rode on.

He saw the campfire and heard voices. He also saw the steep overhanging rock. There was another just below it, slightly off the trail, and it stuck up at an acute angle in another direction. It was much smaller than the rock that overhung the campfire.

Brad counted three men who were standing there, warming their hands over the fire.

He rode above the large rock and dismounted. He was sure that none of the men had seen him. And they had probably not heard his shot since there was still the peal of thunder that masked many lesser sounds.

He walked back down to the trail where he could see the three men.

He spotted Schneck. He did not recognize the other two men.

They were still talking. Brad hunkered down and watched them.

The fire burned low. One of the men walked away. He met another man, and they walked down to where Brad could see a bunch of cattle huddled in a tight bunch. They walked past them and climbed onto horses. They rode off and disappeared behind slanted slashes of rain.

Finally, the man who was still with Schneck said something and walked out from under the overhang. He walked down the trail and when Brad next saw him, he was on horseback, heading toward the gathered herd of cattle.

Brad shook his rattle.

Schneck whirled and grabbed for his pistol.

Brad rattled again.

Schneck pulled his pistol from his holster and ran from

under the rock. He ran across the trail and clambered up the other rock.

"Who's that?" he called out.

Brad shook the rattles again, then ran up behind the over-hanging rock. He ran to its edge and looked down at Schneck on the smaller outcropping.

Once again, he shook the rattles and he saw Schneck's head turn and then tilt back to look up.

A flash of lightning silhouetted Schneck and made Brad's form stand out like a sore thumb.

Schneck pointed his pistol at Brad.

"You bastard," he said.

Brad cocked both hammers of the shotgun.

"See this, Schneck?" Brad held the shotgun slightly to one side, the barrels pointing directly at Schneck.

"You got a shotgun. But you came to the wrong place, Detective."

"What does it look like?" Brad asked. "Look close at the two barrels."

"So, it's a sawed-off. So what?"

"You're looking at snake eyes, Schneck."

"What? Are you crazy?"

"Snake eyes. That means you lose, Schneck."

Schneck took deadly aim with his pistol. He squinted as he lined up his sights.

Brad tugged at one trigger of the shotgun and then the other in rapid succession.

Double-ought buckshot spewed from both barrels following the loud duo of explosions. Shots whistled through the air like a swarm of angry bees. The buckshot smashed into Schneck's torso, riddling him with holes from the lead pellets.

Schneck danced like a human contortionist for a half second.

He screamed like a woman.

He fired his pistol, but the bullet shot off at a crazy angle and smacked into a puddle of rainwater.

Schneck screwed himself into a tight, writhing ball and tumbled from the rock. He landed on his head, and Brad heard the crack as his neck broke.

Just as if he had been hanged from a gallows.

Brad cracked open the barrels of the Greener and the shells ejected, striking the rock with a brassy clatter. He reached in his pocket and took out two more shells and loaded them into the empty barrels. Then he snapped the shotgun closed and waited.

Three men rode up and saw the body of Schneck lying there with his neck broken, his shirt and trousers bristling with tufts of torn cloth.

The men looked up at Brad. He stood there with the shotgun as if he were out bird hunting.

"Schneck was a murderer," Brad said, as the rain lessened. "If he had surrendered to me, he would have been tried and hanged. Any questions?"

The three men shook their heads.

"Then, get back to your cattle, and if you want my advice, you'll drive them back to Wyoming. They won't be welcomed up in sheep country."

One of the men, Loomis, opened his mouth to say something in protest, but thought better of it and remained silent.

Brad watched them all turn and go back to the herd.

He hefted the shotgun and walked off the huge rock and down to his horse. He wiped the barrels.

"Snake Eyes," he said as he slipped the Greener back in its case.

He rode toward Denver as the black clouds sailed past the city and brought rain to the long prairie. He was finished with the Denver Detective Agency. He would see Pendergast in the morning, and then he would ride home. Home to Felicity and his own cattle.

Home. The sweetest sound in the English language.

Don't miss the best
Westerns from Berkley

LYLE BRANDT
PETER BRANDVOLD
JACK BALLAS
J. LEE BUTTS
JORY SHERMAN
DUSTY RICHARDS

penguin.com